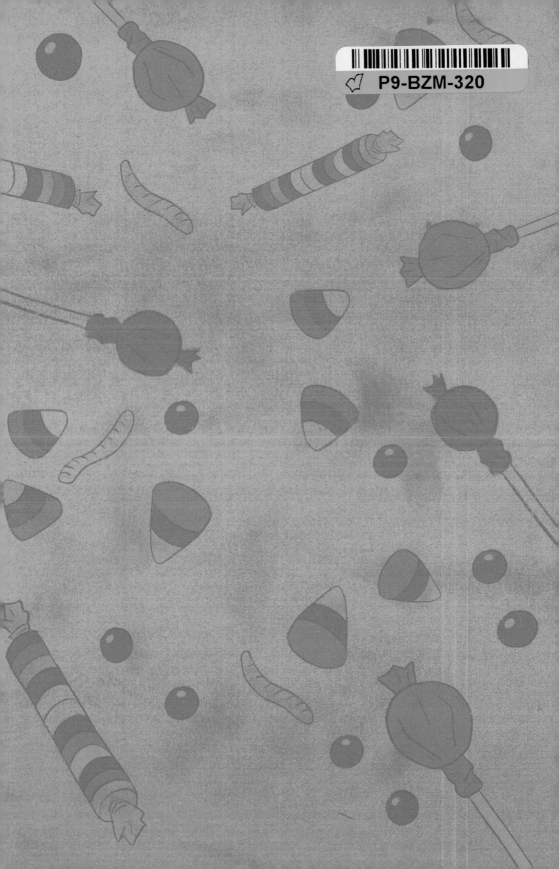

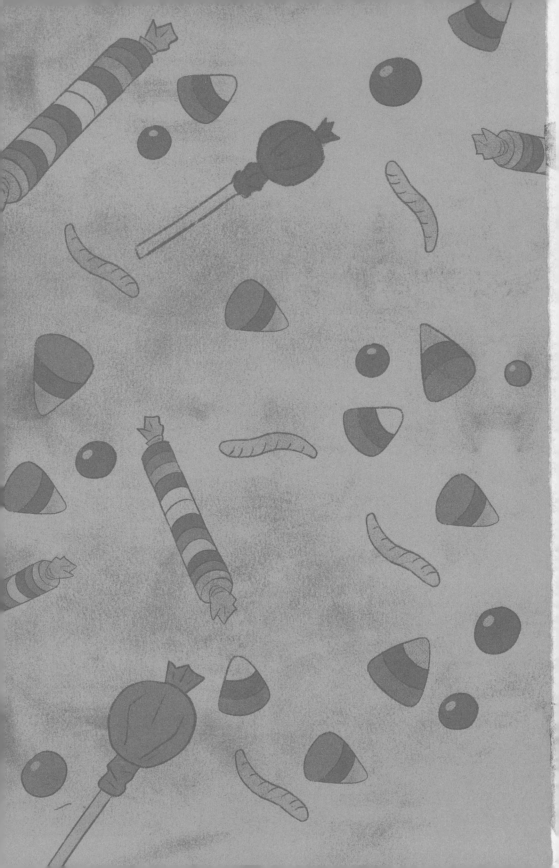

CONFESSIONS
OF A CANDY
SNATCHER

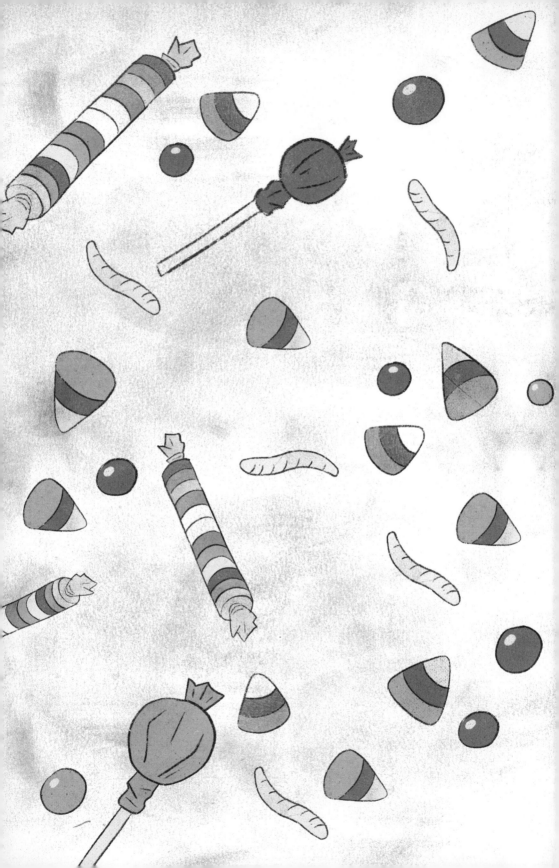

CONFESSIONS OF A CANDY SNATCHER

PHOEBE SINCLAIR

ILLUSTRATED BY
THEODORE TAYLOR III

CANDLEWICK PRESS

First edition 2023

Library of Congress Catalog Card Number 2022908654
ISBN 978-1-5362-1368-3

23 24 25 26 27 28 APS 10 9 8 7 6 5 4 3 2 1

Printed in Humen, Dongguan, China

This book was typeset in Sabon.
The illustrations were created digitally.

Candlewick Press
99 Dover Street
Somerville, Massachusetts 02144

www.candlewick.com

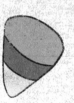

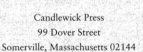
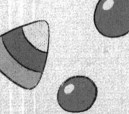

MIX
Paper | Supporting
responsible forestry
FSC® C144853

A JUNIOR LIBRARY GUILD SELECTION

To the naughty ones
PS

To my son Theo
for kindly sharing his
Halloween candy with me
TT III

C: Here's the thing you wanted. You can stop bugging me now. Some of us have our own homework to do. —J

CONTRARY TO POPULAR OPINION

Contrary to popular opinion, I didn't keep all the candy for myself. Most of it, I gave to Rex. I know Mikey sells his. Probably back to the kids he stole it from in the first place.

Snatching is something you do on Halloween if you're big enough. You don't hurt anybody, just get their candy. Then, once you've grabbed it, you run REALLY fast. Most trick-or-treaters won't chase you because they're too scared. That's the other part of snatching: spookin'. If you can't scare people, then you have no business being out there.

The other great thing about snatching is that it's like games on TOP of games. It's a real competitive thing. For example, first person to snatch from a pirate gets dibs on the biggest piece of candy from the other snatchers' stash. Or last person back to base has to run up to a house with a light on, ring the bell, and moon the front door.

I learned how to snatch from my boy Mikey, who is all right at it. Mikey learned from his older brother, who was a pro and retired because now he's too old. Me, Mikey, Darius, and our friend Aaron have been snatching since sixth grade.

My conclusion is that snatching is a serious fun activity if you like to go out on Halloween but don't wanna mess with eggs or toilet paper, and can't see walking around like a schmo, begging for candy. Plus, nobody ever actually gets hurt.

Chapter 1
THE NOTE

At ten-minute recess on Monday, me and the boys horsed around playing something Mikey Hill made up that was near impossible to win, like usual. Most of the seventh graders on the playground wore their thick jackets, and the girls huddled, watching while talking out the side of their mouths. Group of lil' kids nearby in the tot lot fussed, but nobody had their name called by the teacher twenty times, so I knew it wasn't my sister's second-grade class.

Wap! A dull, multicolored Super Ball hit the pavement, then bounced high over our heads. Darius Delicious jumped to double-hand throw a kickball at the receding Super Ball, looking sorry with his pudgy belly bouncing under his coat.

From my seat on the low wall that separated the big kids from the lil', I watched Mikey sneak looks over at the girls. The school behind us was a shadow; some of the trees still wore orange and yellow and brown, the rest naked, probably wanting some snow at least, to cover up with.

MISS! Mikey blurted, trying to make Darius fumble.

Darius said, Man! and cut his eyes at Mikey as he hustled to catch the bright red kickball before it rolled out toward the teachers' parking lot.

You ain't even right, he grumbled.

I couldn't say it mattered much, Mikey trying to psych him out. Darius is tons better at finishing his homework on time and not sharing the answers than at sports.

Aaron, hanging with his skater crowd, snagged the ball as it rolled past. Matching in white and red down to his socks, with medium skin like mine, Aaron came over to bump fists with us, then patted his fade. Darius Delicious did the same with his 'fro, the two of them speaking some secret hair language.

My turn, I told Aaron as I slid from the wall and reached to take the kickball.

Mikey looked at me. He said, What? You had a go before Double D.

I looked right back, said, Taking my second turn. C'mon. Teacher's about to call.

Na-ah. We've got two more minutes, said Mikey.

Didn't check his phone, just pulled that number out of the air.

I was pretty sure we had five minutes left in recess, so I ignored

Mikey, who never wants anyone to win besides his own special self. I started to ask Darius for the Super Ball he held against his hip, but Aaron interrupted, saying, Let me get a go?

I sucked in my sigh. Aaron, too, was checking out Charity O'Dell and her crew, who made like they had other things to do besides watch us. Obviously, they didn't, because they kept turning to stare and giggle.

So I bounce the little one and hit it with the big one? Aaron asked.

Yeah. While they're in midair, Darius said, still puffing from jogging after the ball. You gotta catch at least one.

The Super Ball hit pavement again, louder. I glanced at the teacher, hoping she wouldn't notice us playing with a toy she could confiscate. School hates Super Balls 'cause kids like to throw them in the hall just to see them bounce everywhere, off the lockers, hitting girls.

Both balls flew wild, and Mikey cackled, What the eff? What was that?

The teacher glared in our direction and snapped, Language!

Her breath puffed in the cold air as she shook her head and went back to checking messages on her phone.

I shook my head, too. Mikey's got a big mouth. I watched him, skinny and light like the sun's always on him, thick cornrows braided by his sister. He had his eyes pasted to the ball bouncing lower and slower, and Charity's crew had their eyes on him. I made sure to get to the Super Ball before Mikey.

Naw, man, come on, Mikey complained after I won the race. You took two turns already.

One, I corrected. You can't count?

Because I half turned to face the girls, they shouted, Heeeey, Jonas!

Someone calls your name, it's hard not to look. I spotted Charity O'Dell: pink puffy jacket, pink hat, pink-and-white high-tops. Smacking on gum like it was her job. I didn't bother to respond, just turned back to the boys.

The girls said in unison, Ooooooh!

One laughed. No, he *didn't* just do that!

No time left to waste, I braced myself, calculating distances and speed, stuff like that.

Uh-oh, I heard Aaron hoot. Look at him. Jonas 'bout to show us how it's done!

What's Jonas got to show? Mikey sucked his teeth.

I bounced the Super Ball, hard. It shot way up: a colorful star, a comet, a satellite crossing the playground sky. Could barely see it, but I knew my kickball throw was good when the nubby rubber scraped away from my fingertips. Too good. In the collision, the Super Ball didn't gain altitude, or lose—no, it whipped toward Charity's crew, who screamed and ducked.

Flew over them to hit this one kid, reading by herself on the wall, just at the edge of the lot. Ball struck her temple with a *thonk!* that probably everybody heard.

Gideon Rao fell off the wall like a bottle of beer.

Oh, crap, I said.

And then the bell rang.

* * *

Another bad deal with Gideon, I told myself as I stopped by my locker at the end of the day.

I knew I should find her and apologize. Any other person wouldn't have fallen just 'cause she got clocked by a ball, but Gideon was wispy like a twig. Her hair, thick and black, was probably the heaviest thing about her.

I pulled a yellow slip from my pocket and stuffed it in the locker. Mikey's usually the one does something really dumb and gets caught. I bet I wouldn't have gotten in trouble for hitting Gideon if the teacher wasn't already annoyed because of Mikey swearing.

This was my second infraction this month. One more and I'd end up with detention, or school community service.

School had mostly cleared, the last few kids horsing around in the empty-sounding hall and Vice Principal Hong on patrol. As I shoved books in my locker, metal door clanging, VP strolled my way, hands tucked behind her back. She was about as tall as a fifth grader, usually wearing striped suits and with hair like a floppy black V over her forehead.

As VP passed, she smiled and nodded at the floor. I looked down.

Oops, I said, grabbing the slip of paper at my feet.

I started to unfold it. It was probably from Charity O'Dell's girls; her crew was big into stuffing notes through the slits of my locker.

I KNOW IT WAS YOU.

Cold air from nowhere ran its fingers up my spine, like someone opened a window and let the spooky in.

I KNOW IT WAS YOU.

I flipped the paper over, but there was nothing else. Just those tiny, neat words between blue lines in the middle of a ripped paper square. I turned the note this way and that but didn't recognize the handwriting. I glanced around to see if anyone was watching. A lower-school kid with his mom fast-walked to the stairwell, and a few upper-school girls with duffels *click-click-click*ed their heels toward the gym. Otherwise? No one.

I KNOW IT WAS YOU.

I pushed down the buzzing in my pulse.

I KNOW IT WAS YOU.

Gotta be Mikey, I decided. He's been a joker since we met in kindergarten. Me and Double D learned early: laugh with Mikey instead of getting mad and he'll have your back something fierce.

I crumpled the note, tossed it back on the floor, and kicked it away from my locker so VP Hong wouldn't write me up for littering on school property.

* * *

C. & I lounged on her sun porch with windows shut tight as we could make 'em, cold air seeping in around the edges. Nothing seemed important enough to hurry.

We sprawled on the dusty floor, work spread out. I leaned back against an old rocker, edge of the wooden seat getting me in the ribs, but not enough to make me move.

Glad to be sitting around just doing boring ol' math, I said on cue when C.'s bright blue eyes landed on me after a long explanation of her mother's latest research breakthrough or whatever.

She blinked slowly, with attitude, like, Yeah, you BETTER have been listening.

C. moved to North River to live with Rodrigo, her mom's brother, because her mom is a journalist who follows the most dangerous stories possible—like this new one about how kids our age get stolen and sold around the world. Cool job, but C. usually can't go with her mom. She travels a lot with Tío Rodrigo, who also studies stuff, but in places that have more dust than danger.

Instead of starting in on those last two problems, I tapped my pencil lightly against the side of my sneaker and watched C. place a stencil in a wood frame over some paper, squirt a glob of blue ink from a tubby bottle with a nozzle, and then scrape the ink with a squeegee. She sat back and lifted the stencil, pulling her lips to one side. I almost smiled at the funny face she made, big ol' eyebrows low.

Sometimes I'd be blathering on about an annoying chore my parents were on me to do, or some wackness my sister Rex swore totally happened to her (yeah, in her *imagination*), or what new prank Mikey took up that put us *all* in it with VP Hong, and C.'d look like she wasn't paying a lick of attention. Then she'd say somethin', one lil' thing that didn't even seem important, but I'd feel my shoulders sink, back of my neck loosen. And I'd be like: Oh. I hadn't seen it that way.

C. placed a second framed stencil over the same sheet of paper, squeezed the red ink too hard, and blew the lid off.

Giiirl, I muttered, rubbing a red spot off my sneaker. C.'d gotten the seat of the rocker, too, and the white wood-panel walls, and a stack of lumpy things beneath old sheets, five feet away.

We inspected the splatters, checking our clothes and glancing around the porch. At my place, Mom would blow two tons of screaming if Rex or me dripped ink on our deck. Probably have us scrubbing it with our toothbrushes.

What're you trying to make? I asked.

Mierda, C. said, lifting the screen to inspect the picture beneath. Crooked.

I met Concepción two years ago in a ridiculous Bees 'n' Trees class Mom signed me up for at the Nature Center. When the instructor teamed us up, I remember shaking my head at the short, hook-nosed girl with dark curling hair that she kept stuffing back in her hoodie. She grabbed the assignment out of my hands and hissed in her Chilean accent, Gonna blow through this!

C. had me running: two hours' worth of trees identified in twenty minutes. Spent the rest of that class sucking down honey sticks that were supposed to be everyone's rewards, and not reading about indigenous local pollinators, whatever those are.

Okay, Jonasito, said C., like she'd answered my question. Here's where you come in.

She scooted over, sitting so our knees bumped. I checked my phone, figuring she was about to explain a project her homeschool-co-op-class-thing handed out. Before C. I'd never heard of homeschool, and now I knew it meant lessons could sneak up on you at any moment. Time to make my exit.

¡Ojo, presta atención! C. said, smacking the floor loudly with her palm.

I jumped. You have to do that?

Listen, she said, this is a zine. She held up the inked paper, curling in on itself.

C. explained, Zines are like magazines, but cooler, right? They're from THE PEOPLE. They're words and art about important things.

A magazine? I said, waving my hand at all her inks. That what you're working on over there? Ever heard of this thing called the internet?

C. sucked her teeth and said, You can't hold a website in your hands. You can't take a website to the revolución.

I almost rolled my eyes. C. could be a factory of wacky ideas about changing the world and bringing peace to THE PEOPLE. I considered repeating some of what I heard on the radio about folks using social media to overthrow governments. Then I decided, Nah.

I smiled. You startin' the revolución with one sheet of paper?

This is just the cover, she said. I'm still figurin' out the design, but I already got the topic. You can write—you're good in English. Get your friends to help, you know the ones you never bring over?

I pulled a face. C. and the boys together? That'd be a nightmare. She and Mikey would go at it!

Gotta jet, I said, and started to pull my things together.

She said, You're gonna write for the zine?

I laughed. I don't write for fun.

You don't want to know what it's about? C. asked.

Nope, I said, stuffing my backpack.

I stood. In November, night comes on quick. The sun pushed lines through the blinds. Throwing shadows, Dad calls it. Stripes of light and dark across C.'s face, hoodie, pale hands as she stood, too, top of her head about level with my nose. The blinds rattled with a cold gust, light and dark swinging.

She said, You, Jonasito, are gonna write about the WORST thing you ever did.

I felt my heart squeeze. Once, real fast. Glad I didn't mention that note in my locker.

I blinked. Laughed again and said, What? No way.

It was kind of a fake laugh.

Chapter 2
WATCH YOUR BACK

WATCH YOUR BACK, said the second note.

Just Mikey trying to mess with your mind, I told myself as I jammed the scrap of paper into my coat pocket and continued moving books and notebooks from locker to backpack. Straightening, I twirled my lock and then jumped about a mile when Mikey himself slapped me on the back, hooting, Jone, Joni, Jonas!

Jeez, I said as I flicked my eyes at him.

Darius drifted next to us, careful-slow with a far-off expression on his face like every step was an answer to some brainy question the rest of us didn't even know to ask.

Man, when are you going to get rid of that stupid hood? Mikey said, elbowing him. You look like a freakin' Eskimo.

Darius's black-brown eyes lifted to watch the fur on his jacket hood wave its fingers like one of those not-plants-exactly from the bottom of the ocean. He shrugged.

Inuit, Darius corrected. Yup'ik, or you could say Alaska Native.

We stared at him.

Eskimo's the white man's word, he told us. Like Negro.

Mikey and me sort of blinked, and then Mikey asked me, You coming with us to Mr. Pizza?

How long you going for?

Mikey shrugged. You got someplace to be?

Uh, *yeah*, I wanted to say. Unlike the boys, I'd been working for money since I was just ten. I couldn't do a lot of hours, of course, but what used to be me hanging at Mom's shop 'cause that's where my parents were turned into small jobs, and then putting in time every week. When we went to do stuff, like hit the arcade or grab a slice at Mr. Pizza, I did the paying since Mikey never had any money and Darius saved his allowance to buy new comics and games that he traded with us later.

As we walked toward the exit, Darius filled us in. He said, Charity O'Dell and them said they'd be there.

Maaaan, I said as I readjusted the straps of my backpack to fit around my thicker coat. Y'all going to Mr. Pizza to hang out with those *girls*? I'm good. I gotta get to Soho anyway.

Mikey sucked his teeth. I don't get why Charity's crew is into you. You don't never want to do nothin' fun, but they're like, Jonas coming? Where's Jonas?

Mikey thinks Charity O'Dell is the prettiest girl in our class; all I know is she's the loudest. You have to watch her; she'll diss you same time she's smiling your way. On the other hand, as the biggest busybody in seventh grade, if anyone had clues about who'd been visitin' my locker, might be her.

I frowned, glancing sideways at Mikey. I said, You mean fun like leaving creepy notes in people's lockers?

He said, What?

I took the scrap from my pocket and pressed it against the front of Mikey's too-thin jacket.

Joke's up, I said, and grinned so he'd know I was in on the prank.

We stopped just inside the school doors. Cold air swept inside in waves as people around us banged in and out of the building.

Darius peering over his shoulder, Mikey read the note. Four eyes snapped to mine, and I didn't see what I hoped in any of them.

Mikey made a face. He said, This ain't mine.

Darius craned his head around at a sound. He hissed, Look fast—
here comes VP Hong.

We hightailed it, heading out the green double doors that opened
to the front lawn of North River K–8 and the circular drive where
cars waited, parents inside looking annoyed. We joined the kids
headed to the crosswalk, a sea of hoods, sneakers, and boots.

I told Mikey, I knock a girl over with a ball and a mysterious note
shows up. Ooooh. Who could it be? The girl? Is it the boogeyman?

I meant to be funny, but Mikey stopped before we hit the crosswalk. A few eighth-grade guys bumped him in passing and he
didn't threaten them behind their backs like usual.

Mikey said, Not my fault you guilty.

Whoa. I stopped, too. Mikey had sworn, Darius had sworn, even
Aaron Camp—who had been with us earlier on Halloween night—
when we'd told him after, held up his palm and promised. Unless
we were tucked away in Darius's basement or some other secret
place, we wouldn't say a word about anything that happened when
we were candy snatching.

I closed in till we were eyeball to eyeball, me looking up some.
Mikey didn't say anything, but his nose flared, his chin eked an
inch higher. Those green eyes the girls giggle over, narrowed and
glinting.

Told myself, Not worth it. Mikey's always spoiling; he'd as soon fight you as laugh with you.

Not my fault you're a killer, Mikey said, breath smelling like those peanut butter and Fluff sandwiches he eats too many of.

Heat dropped from my chest to my fists. My hands throbbed to pop him.

Hey. C'mon. Darius tried to push between us, but we pressed toward each other like magnets.

You should show this to VP, Darius said, pulling the note from Mikey's hand to read for himself. I mean, what if it's serious?

Darius has never been a fighter. He was probably picturing some-one pulling up in a pickup truck, headed for my locker with an automatic, but couldn't be anybody mad at me who didn't go to NR K–8 or live in my own house. I knew the notes had to be com-ing from close by.

Still . . . the Dad in my head told me: throw a fist and everybody loses.

Double so with Mikey. We've rumbled a few times. Goose punches or a knee to the gut getting lost in the puff of too-big jackets. Finally, I huffed air from my nose. Stepped back. Maybe Mikey wasn't behind the notes, or maybe he wanted to keep messing with me until he got bored.

I plucked the note from Darius's stubby fingers. When I tossed it, the wind took it and blew out a question. Too bad I didn't have the answer.

*　*　*

I hauled open the door, fighting wind that tried to jam it closed, and crossed the front of Soho Stationery. Dodged a box left out on the floor before squishing myself behind the L-shaped checkout counter next to Stewart Ko's beanpole self.

Yo, little man, Stew said in greeting, flipping red-dyed hair out of his eyes.

Soho Stationery is one of the smallest shops in downtown North River. Work or school or weddings, people purchase paper and office supplies to their heart's content. High school punks come for fat Sharpies or fine-point pens to draw on their own arms and legs. Jersey Shore tourists like the rainbow umbrellas and sailboat paper mobiles dangling in the front windows. Once Stew and me caught Mikey and Darius racing out, leaving a line of plastic windup rabbits, chicks, and turtles crashing, one by one, over the edge of the checkout counter.

I grunted in Stew's direction and snagged my clipboard of tasks from its cubby under the counter. As I scanned the short list, the leather strap of sleigh bells still on the door from two Christmases ago clanged, and a short lady in black slipper-shoes walked in. No reindeer, but the chill followed her in.

Stewart met the woman out on the floor, and they walked over to shipping supplies, speaking in Korean. I couldn't understand the words, but listening to their low voices calmed me.

What's new? Stewart said as he returned to ring up bubble envelopes for the wrinkle-faced, white-haired lady, who stared at me with a blank expression. Just her eyes moving, following Stew and me.

I shrugged.

What's your homeschool buddy up to this week? Stew tried again over the sound of the register coughing up a slip of blocky numbers.

After the lady left, he went for a third. He asked, Any wacky projects that you need my brilliant suggestions for?

Stew has known me long enough you'd think he'd stop asking questions when it's obvious I'm not talking. He was our babysitter when Rex was tiny and Mom and Dad worked all the time to open the shop. When he started at college for photography, Stew picked up hours at the Soho and now he's a manager. The old Korean ladies who come in for mailing supplies constantly try to get him to date their lawyer daughters. We laugh about it and never mention his pro-skater boyfriend.

I thought about C.'s zine and the story I wasn't planning to tell— nohow, thanks, anyway.

On the other hand, what would one question hurt?

Hey, I said. What's the worst thing you ever did?

Without changing his expression, Stew walked over, picked up the left-out box, and moved it next to one of the circular racks at the front. He started filling the rack with postcards from the box, unwrapping the plastic and letting it fall to his feet.

How much time do you have? he asked.

Really? I said.

He thought for a minute. Are you more interested in my elementary, middle, or high school years?

I said, I dunno. Middle school?

Stew added, You want drugs, scars, or police arrests?

My mouth dropped open.

Then I laughed. I know you! You can't have been all that bad.

Raised by wolves, he said proudly, rolling up his sleeves.

Tattoos, starting at the wrists, disappeared up into his shirt. On one arm, a small boat riding the stormy sea inside a black clay pot, and the other a collection of bands, thick and thin. I remembered tracing the bands when I was, like, bitty Jonas, my fingers going 'round and 'round his tan-gold skin. Light and dark.

Polite, organized wolves. Stew grinned. No, I lie. My parents are very traditional. I'm the wolf.

I'm the wolf, I told myself. With my boys, chasing kids down the street to steal their candy.

Why do you ask? Stew said, finally serious.

No reason, I said, shrugging, and went to restock the binders. Alone in my head, I watched Gideon chase Mikey chase Halloween chase a big ol' pile of trouble. If Gideon told, that was . . . I'd get in it BIG with my parents, maybe tossed right out of school. Still, it was hard to see her doing that now, after so much time had passed.

Later, after a few more customers came and went, after I took over the postcard job, I called across the store.

So, C. wants me to write for her new zine thing.

I was about to explain what a zine is when Stew called back, Oh, yeah? I made a few in my day.

I glanced up. For real? You still have 'em?

Stew said, You don't want to read them. You're thinking naughty, but it's more like nerdy. How about this: I'll let you in on a great zine-making secret?

I shook my head. Nah.

Well, that's just too bad. Stew drifted over to the stockroom door and beckoned me. C'mon.

I glanced behind at the empty store. Dark night outside punched with light from the streetlamps.

In the stockroom, everything felt quiet and still. Smelled both dusty, like old cardboard boxes, and clean, like new glossy paper. I tried to find some place to stand that wasn't crowded with boxes as Stew dug beneath a folding table. The pile on top wobbled, and I batted aside a small box that nearly hit him when he stood.

Weird how crazy-messy Mom is at work, I thought. But then has a fit if I leave my cup next to the sink at home for more than five seconds.

Thanks for the save, Stew said, carefully setting something on a corner of the table. This thing probably has you by fifty years, but I think you're going to dig it.

Musical instrument? I wondered, peering at the flat, trapezoid-shaped box. Atari? A vintage game system would be awesome.

My guess, said Stew, is that this has been here from *before* the shop that came *before* Soho.

He pressed two tabs at the front with his thumbs and snapped the lid off.

We stared at the gleaming pink machine. Not any game system I ever saw.

Stewart pressed a floating button with a black **Z** on it. *CLAK!*

The noise made me step back. Stew grinned.

This is my favorite part. He raised his voice as he pressed letters rapid-fire. *CLAKCLAKCLAKCLAKCLAKCLAKityCLAKCLAK-CLAKCLAKCLAKCLAK! ding.*

Stewart pushed a shiny **L**-shaped lever and slid the black tube back to its original position on the left. *Krrriiiit!*

He said, Now we're ready to write the next line. The typewriter is THE zine-making machine. In my opinion, second in importance only to the copier.

Oh, no, I realized. He's going to make me take it.

Keep it yourself, or give it to your friend, Single Initial. She'll love you forever.

Or she can use a computer like a normal person? I said, inching backward. I told her she should just start a blog.

Nope. Stewart shook his head. Not the same.

I asked myself, How can I get out of this without seeming rude?

I don't think I can carry it, I lied, eyeing the pink machine.

Probably weighs a ton, I thought. All that metal.

Don't worry, I'll drop you home after I close up here, Stew assured me.

While I was fixing my face to look less annoyed, Mom poked her head around the stockroom door. There you are!

Hey, Ms. Adams. Stew smiled as Mom picked her way through the clutter.

Nice dye job, Mom said, glancing at Stew's hair as she patted hers down into place. Even though she refuses to let Rex get her hair straightened, Mom spends about a bajillion dollars on hers to keep it loose and shiny. She calls it a "business expense."

She added, And I hope you have a good reason why you're back here instead of up at the front, greeting customers.

She eyed me until I turned my face up. I managed not to squinch my eyes when she kissed my cheek, but somehow she could still tell.

Mmm, she said. Fresh.

A fantastic reason! Stewart told her, taking her peacoat at the navy-blue elbow and moving her closer to the table.

Dude has never been smart enough to be afraid of Mom, I told myself as they leaned forward.

I'm going to give this old typewriter I found to your son, Stew said. Just think of it. One less item clogging your stockroom.

Mom made a face. She said, And one more cluttering my house.

*   *   *

After dinner, I engaged in a backpack excavation, hanging over the edge of my bed with both arms deep in the bag. I had already pulled out more books and crumpled sheets of paper than should have been able to fit, not one of them what I was searching for.

Somewhere under the paper and books, or maybe beneath the dirty clothes, or possibly behind a stack of video games I'd been meaning to trade, my phone croaked a text alert. I interrupted the homework search for a brief phone search, and then I quit both. I groaned, dropping my face into the dusty folds of the thing Mom calls a "bed skirt" and I call "pointless."

Time for a ten-minute sweep.

Even though our house is a decent size, Rex and me have small bedrooms. We're on the second floor (Mom has a bigger bedroom downstairs), and at night, with the shades down and slanted ceiling, my room can feel closed in, like a cave. Unlike Rex or Mom, I have three windows, which is cool because I can look between the narrow trees at a creek that runs behind the houses. In the summer, I hear frogs peeping. Once I saw an owl.

I forward-rolled off the bed with a thump and stepped over Mount Clothingmore to pluck my alarm clock off my desk. Standing mid-room, I set a timer. My black mollies, Alex and Swimmy-Lionni, drifted to the front of their little tank to watch the action unfold.

Okay, focus. Time was ticking. I hooked the lip of my recycling bin with my toes and dragged it close, then bent and started shoving things in, not bothering to check what they were. The blue bin was full before I found my phone again under one of Mom's yoga magazines, beneath a dirty pair of jeans.

I responded to the text from Darius about plans for a movie marathon with Mikey and maybe Aaron, and reached to drop the yoga magazine in the recycling. I knew I should take it back downstairs, but I didn't feel like it. Last summer, Mom started taking Rex (never me) to class with her every week. Whatever—not like I wanted to be in a room full of sweaty people with their butts in the air, anyway. Another item sticking out of the bin caught my eyes: one of the zines C. had loaned me. Right before I ran outta the house to escape her wack assignment, she'd shoved one at me, and I couldn't leave it behind unless I wanted to get a text avalanche from the girl later.

Glanced at the clock: five more minutes. I speed-flipped through the zine so I could say I'd read it. Words crowded together in a blocky font that was hard to make out. The pictures were black-

and-white, some drawn by hand, some blurry like they were photo-copies of photocopies of photocopies.

See? I thought. A blog would be a whole lot easier to read . . . I paused at a picture that reminded me of Rex, a little girl smirking and wearing star-shaped sunglasses too big for her face. The poem beneath was short enough. I read it.

A Recipe for Disaster—Ingredients:

Me and my sister
Car
Hot day, sun
Dad up front
Long ride
Four cigarettes
Nothing to do

Funny, I thought, but something didn't seem right, so I read it a second time.

Me and my sister
Car
Hot day, sun

I'd been there. Rex bored and annoying me till I was ready to stran-gle her. Mom belting along to gospel on the radio like wasn't any-one else in the car.

Dad up front
Long ride

If Dad wasn't driving, back when he lived with us, he'd read his paperwork, distract Rex, and keep Mom laughing, all at the same time. My parents acted like goofy kids, snort-laughing and setting word traps and teasin'.

Read the poem a third time:

Four cigarettes
Nothing to do

Somebody is about to get smacked! More I thought about it, the more the poem didn't seem funny. I closed the zine and peered at the front cover: a big blank except for the title of tiny square handwriting that reminded me of the threat notes from my locker.

I tossed the zine on my desk and the alarm started to beep slowly. I knew it would annoy my mother if I didn't turn it off soon.

From downstairs, I heard my mother call, muffled, What's that beeping? Jonas? Roxanne?

It's not me! Rex called back.

Slumping down on my bed, I threw an arm over my eyes. I heard my sister start padding around. Since upstairs was just our rooms, a bathroom, and some closets, I knew she'd appear in my doorway soon enough.

Jonas! my mother shouted again.

The alarm started beeping faster. Eventually, it would turn itself off. My room was still kind of a mess.

Rex's head appeared around my door as Mom continued hollering for me to kill the noise. Seven-year-old self too old for footie pj's but wearing them anyway. Puffy braids + big head + round eyes + teensy lips = Roxanne Abraham, who says what she wants, does what she wants, and generally smells like oatmeal cookies (it's the coconut hair grease).

I smiled and pointed to my alarm clock.

Get that? I said.

Rex raised one eyebrow, a funny expression on her baby face.

IT'S JONAS, she yelled down the stairs, and disappeared into the bathroom.

That's how you treat your brother? I said, rolling over, off the bed.

The alarm cut off. I nudged the bin back under the desk with my foot.

Chapter 3
FRESH

On Friday, Dr. Adeyemo handed copies of a pop quiz on integers to the first student in each row.

Does anyone NOT have a pencil? he asked over the chorus of groans and sighs. Okay. There's nothing on this quiz that you haven't seen. If you were paying attention on Monday, Tuesday, Wednesday, or Thursday, you'll be fine.

When Darius passed back a quiz, I caught sight of Mikey looking our way from two rows over. Probably wishing he was close enough to copy answers.

Back at the front of the room, Dr. Adeyemo smoothed his yellow dashiki and checked his watch. You've got twenty minutes. If you finish early, please put your pencils down and sit quietly.

I reviewed the questions and nodded to myself. Cake. Hanging weekly with C. to do homework (my idea that Mom went batty for after that Nature Center class; for some reason she didn't think it was strange that I wanted to hang out with some weirdo homeschool kid) made surprises like pop quizzes a lot less scary. After a bit of quick work, I moved on to the more pressing problem of sleuthing out the mystery notes in my locker. I could just *feel* another one coming.

I took out blank paper, waiting to see if Dr. Adeyemo would say, Chill. He stared dreamily out the window, so I took the opp to pull a Truman (as Mom likes to say about Dad's thing for writing out lists) and brainstorm what I should do about the mystery notes.

First, a list of the people who might bank on me having a freak-out:
   -Mikey
   -Charity O'Dell (who knows?)
   -Charity's girls (likely)
   -Gideon
   -Gideon's brother (ninth grader—he even know who I am?)
   -Darius (unlikely, though he is a great accomplice)
   -Aaron (for why?)

Next I wrote out the bad stuff that could happen to me:
   -Suspended or, worse, in-school suspension
   -Parents find out
   -Lose privileges (such as doing whatever I wanna every Friday afternoon, except if I have detention, which is only once in a blue moon and always because of Mikey)
   -Dad disappointed
   -Mom ballistic
   -Get arrested????
   -Go to Juvie

-Jail break
-Hop freight trains for the rest of my life and live like a hobo
-Eat a lot of stolen apples

Finally, I listed ideas about how to avoid most of the stuff on my second list:

-Find out who is leaving the notes and make them stop
-Preemptively (A++ for vocab word use!) run away and live like a hobo

I tried again:

-

Sighing, I stretched and looked around. Darius, also done with the quiz, was reading a paperback, but Mikey still seemed hard at work. Outside, cars drove back and forth in front of our school. While I watched them, the poem in the zine that C. lent me popped into my head: something about a long ride, about cigarettes.

I ripped off a rectangle of paper from the bottom of the sheet I'd been brainstorming on and started to fold. Felt good to get the fingers moving. I turned and tucked as I listened to Mikey sigh and Dr. Adeyemo clear his throat.

Five more minutes, teacher announced.

Gideon wasn't in this class because girl was smarter in math than even Double D. I remembered how she showed up in fifth grade:

skinny black-haired brown girl talking some slow twang. She called her old home the Lone Star State or Don't Mess With and liked to tell how famous musicians used to hang at her house 'cause her dad was In The Business. I remember kids got excited, too, till they realized it wasn't music people like us listened to. I mean, who knew what a sitar was? A tabla?

My hands slowed, and a last tuck turned the strip of paper into a triangular football, ready to flip over a field goal of forefingers and thumbs.

Worst thing I ever . . .

Worst thing I ever did.

Did. What did I do? What happened with Gideon on Halloween wasn't great, but why dwell? The boys and me wrapped up those streets for two years. Running in a pack like wolves. That rush in my chest that made me laugh huge, spit bursting so I had to wipe my mouth, but who cared? Too dark to see.

> Worst thing I ever
> Did was

In fourth grade my class did a unit on poetry, and my favorites were the haiku: super-shorties from Japan about stuff like mountains and weather. With only seventeen syllables, you could write practically any ol' thing and have it sound sharp. Maybe I'd submit a lil' poem to C.'s zine and be done. (Take back that first piece I scribbled the other day after we wrote persuasive essays in English—too close to home.)

Worst thing I ever
Did was also the most fun

Five and seven. I counted syllables by mouthing the words and letting my chin bump my hand. Needed another five.

And I didn't even get in trouble.

No, not right. And too many syllables. I tapped my eraser against my teeth; tasted as pink as it looked.

And I didn't get caught.

One minute, called the teacher.

Still one syllable over. How 'bout this?

And nobody knows.

Dropped my pencil on top of my turned-over quiz. Okay, wasn't true. Kids at school and in the neighborhood suspected. Even after the first year, in sixth grade, I heard whispering. From the kids; adults seemed pretty dumb. Distracted. My dad never even asked where my costume was when I left the house this year. He was too busy suiting Rex up in the crazy double-helix costume she'd begged him to make.

Worst thing I ever

I lifted my pencil again. Wait long enough and trouble might blow by and leave the good stuff behind, leave what I'd rather remember.

Aaand pencils down, said Dr. Adeyemo.

He stood, adjusting the kufi on his head, and surveyed the room. I quickly put my hand over the football/poem to hide it.

> Worst thing I ever
> Did was also the most fun . . .
> I felt really free.

*   *   *

At the end of the day, I caught up with Mikey and Darius at the crosswalk. The guard with dreadlocks thick as a first grader's arm had busted out a bright yellow raincoat like the kind that marmalade-obsessed bear from the kiddie book wears. He flipped his miniature stop sign toward the cars and motioned to us.

I ducked under Darius's umbrella as walkers lurched forward in a bunch. Rain could freeze your nose off this time of year. Thanksgiving was a few weeks away, and after it'd be all cold, all the time till May.

I said to Darius, Nice sky.

He glanced up at the underside of his umbrella, blue with clouds like a summer day.

Gotta keep it happy, he said.

Look fast, Mikey warned, face mostly hidden under a dripping black hood.

Mikey's oldest sister, who looks after them—his brother, Mikey in the middle, and a ten-year-old sister—would be pissed to see him with no umbrella. He wore the same thin coat all year but kept it looking sharp.

Charity O'Dell's crew appeared beside us and immediately started giggling and carrying on. Here we go, I thought.

When we got to the section of sidewalk where it widened, Mikey shot ahead of Darius and me. Ducking low, he swooped in and popped up under Charity's super-size pink umbrella. Laughter and squeals. I saw Charity swing her giant purse and wallop Mikey.

Eeew, boy! she yelped. Don't touch me!

Mikey moved his arm to Charity's shoulders and reached low to do the same with her buddy (a girl named Gracie, but me and the boys called her Ton O' Braids because her long, heavy braids pulled her head to one side), who barely came up to Mikey's chin.

You like it, Mikey was telling the girls, leaning his weight and picking up his feet so they had to carry him. They all staggered forward. Get OFF, Charity barked. Help!

At her command, two other girls, dressed exactly alike in pink jackets with white rubber boots, scuttled forward, swinging their open umbrellas. It was a battle scene, a whirl of color as cars swooshed past, splashing rainwater up on the sidewalk. I heard Mikey yelp. Luckily none of the other girls had Charity's pipes—she was hollering enough for ten.

Ton O' Braids escaped, dropping back to match our pace. Darius immediately started his quiet-guy thing where he abandons speaking to giggle or nod, so we walked in silence for a few minutes while I tried to think of something to say.

I asked Ton, You headed to Mr. Pizza?

Ton: For a bit. But then I need to pick my brother up from after school.

Darius:

Me: Where's your brother?

Ton (remembering the rain and opening her umbrella with a spray of water that caught Darius and me in the face): KinderCare on Baker Street.

Me: Yeah? My sister went there. Now she goes to the Y.

Darius:

Ton (looking at Darius): Don't you have a sister, too?

Darius: She's older. Next year she's going to college.

Ton: That's cool.

Darius:

Ton:

Darius:

Ton:

When I started feeling like I might throw myself into traffic, or join Mikey's loud fray, Ton turned her magic powers of conversation on me.

Ton: Hey. I heard from Charity that you have a stalker. The good kind, not like with a knife?

Me: (!!!)

Ton: Any guesses who? I can tell you right now, it's not me.

Me (Darius, help me out): That's what people call a rumor.

Darius:

Darius (after I jab him with an elbow): (giggles)

Ton: Well, I bet it's a girl.

Me:

Darius (magically discovering voice): Who's your guess?

Ton: Well, I don't know. I hear a bunch of girls like Jonas, or at least they talk about him.

Me:

Darius (glancing my way): I guess he's only a *little* fugly.

Me (jabs Darius again, harder):

Darius: Ow! Me and Mikey can stake out your locker. Or, get this, I have an old webcam at home and we could install it in a corner, on the inside. The culprit would never see!

Me (Culprit?):

Ton: Your locker, huh? Somebody leaving notes?

Me (side-eyeing Darius): Thanks for giving that away, genius.

Darius: What? We're getting to the bottom of a mystery.

Me: How's a webcam going to take a picture *through* metal? It's not an MRI or whatever. Nobody is opening the locker besides me. (I think. I hope.) You can't see nothing out of those skinny slats.

Darius: I've been inside a locker. You can see good enough.

Ton: (!)

Me: (?)

Ton: Want me to ask around?

Me: No!

Darius: The villain will reveal their identity eventually. Probably in a series of funny events, like that play my sister acted in last year, *Much Ado About Nothing*. You ever seen it? It's Shakespeare—

Me: Villain?

Me: Could we be walking any slower? I'ma die from starvation.

Up ahead, the battle had ended with Mikey and Charity going off under the umbrella together. Two girls turned down a side street. A third girl twirled a polka-dot umbrella while she pressed a phone to her ear.

Ton: If you're getting these notes 'cause you did something bad, I guess we'll find out. I hope you said sorry. Probably not. Boys don't never say sorry.

Darius: Sexist!

Ton: Anyway, if you don't want notes, just tape a notebook cover or something over the holes in your locker. That's what I'd do.

Me (. . . OMG):

Darius: Huh.

We stopped in the parking lot behind the collection of stores that included Mr. Pizza, a trying-to-be-retro video-rental place that looked ready to go out of business any day, the jewelry shop where Rex and me buy Mom gifts, and that Italian bakery with the pink-and-green leaf-shaped cookies that taste more boring than you'd expect.

I watched Mikey and Charity wander through the cracked and crumbling lot like they were strolling the ashy wood boardwalk planks in the hot summer sun. Like the sky wasn't dumping water on their fool heads. More and more, they annoyed me. Mikey always seemed to want to be around Charity, or have her tag along.

I checked the time and said, I'm gonna get a slice real quick and head home. You in, D?

Darius nodded. I'm texting my mom to come pick me up. You want a ride?

Mikey and Charity had moved under the shops' drippy overhang and were pointing out things in the bakery window. Not once did they look at us. I wiggled my toes in my soggy socks and sneezed. My mind-mama scolded: Walking in the rain? You're going to catch pneumonia!

Ton: I need to get my brother.

Darius: Gracie, um, you sure?

She turned, all those beads clacking: Sure what?

Darius (looking at me for help): Uh.

I found a speck that needed to be rubbed off my sneaker, wet as it was. First Mikey, now Darius. Where would it end?

Darius: Um . . . you don't want to come in for a minute? Split half a pie? We can eat quick.

Ton (sunny smile):

Double D (matching smile all up and down his goofy face):

Me:

At home in the mudroom, I heard Mrs. Delicious's SUV back out
of the driveway. Rest of the house seemed quiet. A pair of Mom's
fuzzy slippers pointed toes-first toward the door like someone set
them up, so I stepped into them. Good fit.

Kitchen was dark, so I hit the switch for the recessed lights over the
counter next to the refrigerator. All the messages Mom left me were
revealed, purple sticky notes in a grid in front of the toaster.

> Jonas—Picking Rex up from
> Friday Swim & going to grab
> a bite. Text when you read
> this so I know you're home.

> Pls take kitchen
> trash out to garage.

I paused to text and wrestle the trash, then returned to read:

> Baby bear: Leftover chicken,
> broccoli, and red bliss in snap-
> top containers in fridge, top
> right shelf. Heat 3–5 minutes.

What's a bliss? I wondered, opening the fridge to inspect Dinner,
the Sequel. Looked like potatoes to me.

Js: Homework IMMEDIATELY
after dinner. No TV. Thank you.
Laptop back in my office
after you're done.

I rolled my eyes. Not only were Mikey and me the only guys I knew without smartphones, but we were also the only ones who didn't have our own laptops at home. Mikey made sense; his family didn't have much. But here I was with two parents in two houses, double the TVs, double the stereos and all that stuffy stuff Mom and Dad like—records, CDs. Sure, I could take my handheld game back and forth, but Mom complained that too much tech corroded us and rationed out the hours, stingy-like. Especially on school nights. *Today's Friday, not a school night, and she's not here, so.*

Js: Remove typewriter to
either your ROOM or TRASH.
Not j/k. FINAL time I'm
going to ask. Thx, luv Mom.

Right. *That.* I turned in a circle till I spotted it on a counter below the cabinets where Mom keeps the fancy plates. The pink trapezoid box was hidden under a pile of mail. I couldn't just throw it out. Thing was a gift. Maybe I'd toss it in the garage or text C. and see if she'd find a use.

While I waited for my chicken to heat, I shuffled over to the typewriter. Like Stew, I pressed my thumbs to the two plastic tabs and popped the lid. The keyboard wasn't much different from a regular laptop, but the rest of the machine could have been from an episode of *Star Trek*. I jabbed keys until the microwave bleated that my food was done.

Red blisses steaming, I dragged the typewriter to the kitchen island and pulled up a stool. Unlike a computer keyboard, the typewriter keys were stiff to press, slow to return to position. I typed my first name. Took a bite. Typed my last name. Took a bite. Typed my full name over and over as I chewed and chewed. When that got dull, I pecked out the alphabet and all the numbers. I was typing the alphabet backward when my mind belched up Stew's words: THE zine-making machine, second in importance only to the copier.

I paused. I swallowed. I typed:

```
worst thing I ever did was also . . .
```

I squinted at the black bar to see if I could spot the dark ink. Chewing open-mouthed for the fun of getting away with it, I returned to the hill of mail, found an envelope addressed to my father, and rolled it on up so it appeared in front of the black bar. Now when I pressed keys, the silver arms rose and fell, creating black block letters like our receipt printer at Soho Stationery.

While I finished eating, I pressed my poem into the back of the envelope.

```
Worst thing I ever
Did was also the most fun
I felt really free
```

Was it fun? After what happened? With Gideon down and me down but my heart up, pounding. Her fists. Her teeth gritted. Streetlight. Black night.

Not after—before. When I was racing through the streets with my boys. Moonlight bouncing off the heads of our prey, like here they are, come get 'em, get 'em!

Yeah. Not after but *before*. Before was awesome.

Chapter 4
TRUE STORY

How should I know if she's leaving you notes? Charity O'Dell snapped when I questioned her in the lunch line. You think I waste my time hanging around your locker?

I said nothing as I followed, grabbing an orange juice carton.

Charity placed two yellow Jell-Os, a milk, and an apple on her tray. Walking so near, I realized we were the exact same height, which was weird. I always thought of her as shorter.

You like her or something? Charity asked.

I wanted to say, Why do you care? But there wasn't enough time. Soon we'd be back out in the lunchroom, where anybody could see us. Obviously, neither of us wanted that.

Enough about your crush, Charity said, wrinkling her nose. I got a question for you, too. About Darius.

Why do you need to ask me for if you can just talk to him? I asked as we skipped some sixth grader who couldn't make a decision.

I *can't* talk to him, she said. Because then he'd *know*.

I bet he knows anyway, I muttered, digging in my pocket for a dollar.

Charity skidded to a halt and stared at me.

What? I asked. You're talking about Ton O' Braids, right? It's obvious . . . and disgusting.

Her NAME'S Gracie, Charity said. And you're disgusting. And stupid.

Yeah, okay, I said, moving to where we needed to pay. This has been a great conversation.

The lunch dude was concentrating on helping Mr. Indecision, who'd somehow passed us, choose between a gross lunch and a grosser one. We had to stand there and wait. Other kids started queuing up behind us. There wasn't much more Charity and I could say to each other without ears hearing, but that didn't stop her from opening her mouth.

Gracie wants to be sure, she said.

We're in middle school, I retorted. What's sure? Nothing's sure.

Okay, Mr. Philosopher, Charity said, and then pressed her lips together, gazing into the lunchroom.

I looked, too. Kids EVERYWHERE. Not a seat empty. Even though North River K–8 switched to sweet potato from regular fries, the ketchup smell was almost overwhelming. Right in the middle, Charity's girls laughed and teased. In the far corner, Mikey and Darius were settling down, probably launching into their daily discussion of the newest handheld games nobody owned yet. And waaaaay over near the exit, Gideon with some thick-legged soccer girls.

Find out what Darius thinks, Charity said. But don't ask him.

What? I laughed. How—?

She said, You and Mikey and him are ALWAYS together. I know you must hear stuff.

I palmed my tiny OJ carton and, giving it a half-hearted toss-n-catch, shook my head. The last thing I wanted was to get mixed up with Charity and them. They'd never leave me alone.

We do have other friends, you know, I said.

The line finally got moving and we both paid.

Sure you do. Charity snickered. Who? Mr. Matches His Hat with His Socks?

I glanced at her pink-pink-pink-as-usual and said nothing as we left the kitchen.

Deal? Charity asked.

I tried to make like a tree, but she grabbed my arm, and of course that was the exact moment Mikey had to look up from laughing with the guys. His eyes went full-floodlight, and Charity tossed my arm away like a fire had exploded between us.

Findmelater, she said out the side of her mouth as Mikey slowly stood up from the lunch table.

Charity called to her buddies and floated in their direction, pretending like she didn't see. Like she didn't care. I didn't want to care either, but as I walked up to our table, Mikey sank into his seat and fixed me with a death stare. The boys around us were yakking, but no way I could play off that cootie exchange with pink-on-pink-on-pink. I plunked down, opened my lunch bag, positioned my OJ while feeling the heat of eyes on my face.

Mikey gets weird about people, I told myself. And whose problem is that?

Not mine.

* * *

What do you want to eat tonight, Littles? Dad asked in the parking lot of the small supermarket near his place.

The sun had pretty much set by five, and since my parents don't *love* me walking around town after dark, Dad drove to pick me up from C.'s. Followed by my sister gabbing from the back seat about how she "helped" Dad at his office and, hey-Joni-did-you-know, a real-live Navy Seal works there now, and Rex walked straight up to the woman and thanked her for her service, like people do on TV news.

I was wondering whether to feel sorrier for Dad or his coworker when Rex bellowed, CANDY!, knowing good and well our parents don't let us eat junk for dinner.

Dad raised an eyebrow at my sister, and two old ladies holding the same shopping cart creaked by and smiled. If I said I wanted candy for dinner, nobody would think it was funny, but Rex gets away with being what Mom calls cheeky.

Light from the front of the store bled out to mix with the street-lamps. I listened to the sound of cars swooshing down the highway behind us as Rex and me trailed Dad through the sliding doors.

Unless he's at work, Dad almost always wears the same thing: dark jeans, a zip-up sweater, leather jacket, square-toed black shoes. Wind walked in with us and tossed his gray scarf as he nabbed a green plastic basket from the stack. In my family, basket = shopping the edges for food that cooks quick: green stuff, probably mushrooms, and something boring / healthy / not frozen for dessert.

How about stir-fry? Dad asked, handing the basket to Rex.

Yuck, Rex said. Can't we have something that tastes good?

We weaved in and out of the crowd, people in the market all at the same time because they're bad at planning ahead, like my family. If I was Dad, I'd go shopping early the nights we stay at his place, especially since he makes his own schedule. I guess he likes to hear us complain twice a week.

You like stir-fry, Dad replied as if he hadn't heard what she said.

Rex rolled her eyes.

They're going to stick like that, I informed her as I followed them to the peppers. To the snap peas. To the mushrooms.

What's going to stick? Rex asked.

Your eyeballs.

Jonas, you're stupid. No, they won't.

I glanced at Dad to see if he'd tell her not to call me names. Nope. Typical.

Yes, they will. I saw it on TV the other night. On the news.

No, you didn't!

I did, too. You wouldn't know because you were already in bed. It was a special segment. This one girl your age had her eyes stuck looking up. She said she was tired of staring at her eyebrows, and at clouds.

Rex started to laugh. She's got this giggle that begins low and then shoots up high enough to crack glass, if she's in the right mood. Before Mom tells us to cool it.

Daddy, Jonas is ly-ing!

Roxanne, choose a different word, Dad muttered.

I could tell he wasn't paying attention as he weighed a big pile of mushrooms and considered, like he'd actually put some back.

Telling stories, Rex corrected herself.

It's true, I went on, widening my eyes and nodding my head slow. The girl on the news will probably need to get eye transplants. Two whole new eyeballs.

Jonas, Dad warned in a low voice as he reached over my shoulder to drop the mushrooms in Rex's basket. Oh, of course he's suddenly paying attention when it's ME.

Dad seemed about to say more, but then his phone rang, so I leaned toward Rex, my own eyes as wide as I could stretch them, hissing, Two. New. Eyeballs!

Daddy! Rex shouted, clutching the basket handle.

Is this necessary? Dad frowned at me, but then he had to answer the phone. Olivia. How's it going?

Mom! Rex squealed, heaving the basket up from where it was nearly touching the floor, even though it couldn't be all that heavy with just a few vegetables.

Dad turned his back to us and wandered a few feet, saying, in a voice I didn't like, No, no, no, it's no problem.

Ugh, I thought.

Rex's eyes followed Dad as he paced near the bagged salads and heads of cabbage. I watched her forget to be freaked out over the dangers of eye rolling.

Here, I said, to distract her, in case the conversation didn't go the way she wanted. (I hoped it wouldn't.)

Rex barely noticed me dumping the bag of mushrooms. I got nearly to the bottom before she interrupted her spying to start ooohing.

I shushed her, plopped a few flat, rubbery mushrooms back in, and jammed the bag into the basket. When Dad turned to check on us, I smiled and waved.

Rex loud-whispered, I'm telling!

No, you won't. You don't like mushrooms, either.

Yes, I do! I like them stuffed with cheese and garlic.

I raised my eyebrows. What? Since when?

Finally, Dad tapped his phone and slipped it into his pocket. He filled a few more produce bags, then hurried us toward checkout, smiling. I frowned. I tried to take the grocery basket from Rex, since it was knocking against her knees. She pulled away, whining, Stoooop, Jonas!

Fine, I said. Break your kneecaps.

I'll break YOUR kneecaps! she barked.

A man walking by looked shocked before he started laughing, but I stepped back because I know Rex bites. When she was little, she was big on going for the knees with her teeth.

Littles, Dad said, catching us both by the nape and steering us into a checkout line. It's been a long day and you're tired, but I need your cooperation. Five minutes, no fighting. You're on the clock.

I asked him, That Mom?

It was, Dad confirmed in a cautious voice.

I groaned, hoping he wouldn't say he'd invited her to dinner, and Dad shot me a quick no-guff glance. Unloading the food while Rex gnashed her teeth at me, he explained, Mommy said she just got word that her meeting is canceled, and she was asking about our plans.

Rex's mood switched instantly. She started cheering. My heart sank, and I tried to think of some way to complain that didn't sound like that's what I was doing. According to the parent magazines Mom kept in a stack on her bedside stand but probably never read, this constant back-and-forth wasn't good for Rex. She was definitely going to grow up screwy.

Dad grabbed two of those expensive chocolate bars that we NEVER buy from the register display and tossed them on the belt.

Who's that for? I asked.

Dad didn't respond other than to raise an eyebrow. I wanted to yurk. He was buying Mom special treats? With eyes everywhere— my dad, the cashier, Grandpa Grocery Bagger—I knew I couldn't sneak and put the chocolate back even if I wanted to, which I didn't because *sugar*.

Groaning, I glanced ahead to a clock hanging at the front of the store, and I saw Gideon. Standing beneath the framed Employees of the Month photos, pink camo backpack hanging off one shoulder, she looked away soon as she noticed me seeing her.

My neck tingled. With the side of my hand, I rubbed under my eye where the bruise and soreness had faded. I wondered if she had hurts, too, that I couldn't see. Probably not. Halloween seemed so long ago.

Last year Rex and I went on a hike early in the morning with Dad in upstate New York, and we saw a white-tailed deer. It was so tall and blowing smoke out its nose, antlers reaching up ragged like branches. Rex thought the deer was on fire. She was afraid it would blow flames all over us, and I laughed. Fire-breathing deer.

Gideon's gaze drifted over, watching me like that deer. Over her head, supermarket Employees of the Month gave somebody (me) the stink eye.

I know it was you.

Rex, leaping for joy in the checkout lane, landed sixty-five pounds on my foot. I gasped, grabbing her arm, and then Dad rushed us and I had to shoulder the goofy reusable bags, and when I glanced over next, Gideon was gone.

* * *

Place smelled like green pepper strips frying and soy sauce.

Jonas! Dad called from the kitchen. Grab some plates. Roxanne, help your brother.

I took my time crossing the five feet between kitchen and living/ dining room. Dad waved a pair of tongs toward the cabinets.

Rex and me took the dishes to the corner under a window where Dad's table sits. A Goodwill find, it's round and wooden with little lines of color where Rex decorated the cracks with marker (she thinks no one knows). First we had to relocate stacks of Dad's work folders, and then I laid out plates, salad bowls, glasses, and paper napkins.

Dad brought over the wok and dropped a big serving on each plate.

He said, I thought I bought more mushrooms than this.

I smiled to myself, then caught Rex squinting in my direction as she came over carrying the big wooden salad bowl. I bugged my eyes huge and leaned into her space. On cue, she whined: Daaaaaad!

Jonas, Dad said, also on cue.

I'd have kept pestering her, but Dad paused, one eyebrow up, and switched tactics.

He said, Tell me one good thing that happened today.

Two can play that game, I thought.

What's the worst thing you ever did? I asked as we settled with our hands cupped, ready to bless the food.

A funny look came over Dad's face, and Rex eyed me with suspicion. Then we all bowed our heads. After, as we served ourselves salad and poured sparkling water, Dad snort-laughed while placing a bread slice on the edge of his plate.

Little man, Dad said, there are SO many things that you will never, *ever* hear about, but I'll tell you one story from when I was around your age. Even when she was younger and feistier, your nana wasn't the type to go shouting, y'know? She'd tell us to go out in the yard and pick a switch.

What's a switch? Rex asked.

Exactly, said Dad. You two don't know how easy you have it.

Easy? I said.

How could he say that as we sat in this condo that Rex and I had helped him choose when our parents decided to trial separate? The place was cool, with its red brick walls and an old metal staircase circling up to a second floor smaller than Mom's bedroom in our original house. I liked the wide windows over bobbing boats on the North River. This place was closer to C.'s and helped us spend time with just Dad. Rex and I had gotten used to it. That didn't mean we loved it, especially not my sister, who watched us with big, watery eyes.

Poor choice of words, Dad admitted.

Two years in, living at two houses isn't any less weird. The parents say they're working on being better friends, but they don't argue less. Even, Mom refuses to give up *Dad's* mom. We see Nana together every few months like nothing's changed. Everything has.

Never mind, I told Dad. I don't need to hear any more.

Jonas, said Dad.

Nope. Game over. I wanted to sink through the floor or rise up, bust through the roof into the sky, and engage a cosmic Ctrl+Z. Redo: take C.'s question and trash it; never ask Dad anything; forget about the zine.

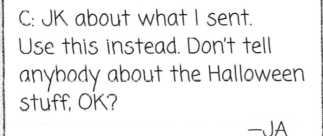

C: JK about what I sent.
Use this instead. Don't tell
anybody about the Halloween
stuff, OK?

       —JA

THAT TIME I LEFT MY SISTER AT MR. PIZZA

The worst thing I ever did was leave
my sister at Mr. Pizza. She was five.

I used to watch Rex three
afternoons a week before I got
a job that pays real money. Me
and Rex were supposed to walk
straight home and start our school
work. Mr. Pizza's on the way, so we
sometimes caught a slice with the boys.
Rex liked to stop. I let her have the soda
refills Dad never does, and also garlic knots.

Mikey was going on about this thing his brother
was into that Mikey wanted us to do in the fall.
Something about candy, but I had a hard time concentrating
because of Rex blowing bubbles in her soda and kicking me
when she swung her legs. She got me one last time on the
shin. It hurt! I remember her eyes wide, straw in her mouth.
Waiting for me to yell.

Mikey was YAK YAK YAK, crunching one peanut
candy at a time, separated into colors, and
Darius had a cheek fulla pizza.

I told my sister, I will leave you here.

And Rex said, Nah-ah.

So I said to the boys, Come on.

She tried to follow when we
left Mr. Pizza, but Mikey and
me held the door. Pizza guy on
the cordless phone watched, but
nobody else came or went. Rex gave
up and sat in the booth by herself.

She wasn't crying,
so I figured she
was okay.

After my boys left, I
popped next door to see
if the store had the new
game I wanted to buy used.
They didn't, and I realized
it was late, so I left real
quick. (Mom explodes if I'm
late for dinner.) Booked it
home, like ten minutes when
usually it takes me fifteen.
Walked in sweating.

Mom was like, Why are you late?

Then I remembered Rex.

Chapter 5
HERE COMES TROUBLE

Here comes trouble, said Stew.

Didn't need ask who he meant. Heard 'em before I saw 'em.

Joni, Jone, Jonas! Mikey bellowed as he and Darius beelined to the tall shelves near checkout where Stew and I were pulling down notebooks to mark for sale.

Luckily, the store was empty while they were stampeding through, crowding the space so Stewart had to make room.

I bumped fists with Mikey, shook Darius's hand, ignored Stew's lopsided, teasing grin.

I can't leave, I warned them. I'm here till five thirty.

Can you talk? Mikey asked, letting his backpack sag off his shoulders and dropping it to the floor.

He can, said Stew. But you'll have to wind him up first.

Mikey went stock-still and frowned, cutting his eyes at Stewart.

Stew, I said.

He held up his hands. Yeah, yeah. I know when I'm not wanted. Come help me finish up the Patrick & Moore letterhead and envelope order after your Trouble Summit, Jonas.

Soon as he left, Mikey shook his body like a dog. Eeeew! Can't believe I had to be next to him.

Darius said, You afraid it's airborne?

Think I can use one of those umbrellas as a homo-shield? Mikey asked.

Both of those idiots laughed and I glared, harder at Darius than at Mikey because I knew D didn't really have issues with Stew. Going along to get along.

Y'all about to leave, I said.

Nobody cared. I glanced to where Stewart had gone, knowing he must have heard, but he never looked up.

Let's sit over there. Darius started toward the wedding nook.

I get the couch! Mikey raced us and got there first, dropping sideways to take up the whole thing.

Door to the shop rang open and a few customers came in. Three ladies who didn't look like they'd be interested in wedding binders, but I took the opportunity to shove Mikey's feet off the couch, harder than necessary.

I narrowed my eyes. When you gonna quit being stupid?

Darius shrugged as he flopped down on the fluffy pink rug, but Mikey gave me a funny look. You know your *friend* over there takes it up the butt, right?

Change the subject before you strangle him, I told myself, sitting beside him in good elbow-to-kidney range.

Darius said to Mikey, Did you remember to bring it?

Mikey pulled a square of paper out of his jeans pocket and flicked it at me.

We found another, Mikey said. Stuck to your locker.

I glanced at Darius. On Monday, he had helped me masking-tape a cardboard notebook cover over the vents in my locker door. Trapped the smell in but otherwise made a decent anti-note shield.

You wrote this, I accused Mikey, still annoyed over him ragging on Stew.

I set the note on my knee, unopened. There was a rolled bit of tape on the back, so it stuck easily. The front said JONAS ABRAHAM, and this time it was printed, like from a computer, not handwritten.

Man, why you keep on with that? Mikey crossed his arms and sat back.

We stared each other down. Darius sighed and wrapped a bit of pink fluff around his fingers.

You're not going to open it? he asked.

Already know what it says, I said.

Mikey broke his silence. D says you think the notes are from that chick. The one you beat up on Halloween? I'd stalk you, too, if I was her.

I took a deep breath. I don't have hundreds of friends. The boys, occasionally Aaron's skate crew, C., Stew, my sister if I need to dig real deep. Folks say I'm quiet 'cause I'm not constantly flapping my lips. No adults would suspect I'm one of the scaries behind the rumors about wolves going full force on Halloween. Sure, kids from school knew: some in my grade, some younger. They stayed away.

Mikey, Darius, Aaron, + Gideon = the only people who knew for sure. But even the boys hadn't seen and didn't know beyond what I told them, which wasn't much.

Don't take the bait, I told myself. Mikey's being mean just 'cause.

I slid a finger underneath the fold and opened the note. Mikey and Darius both leaned forward.

TELL. OR I WILL.

I froze: said nothing, breathed nothing.

Abraham, said Darius. We have a problem.

Mikey snorted. Girl can't say this stuff to your face?

We gotta talk to her, Darius said, All of us together. Or maybe tell somebody, like VP Hong or the principal.

I thawed some, shook my head, and said, No.

He's right, Mikey said. School already knows something happened around trick-or-treatin'. Charity said she heard somebody's dad complaining to VP Hong. We talk about the notes, they'll figure out who's behind snatching and we're busted.

Charity O'Dell, I said. You told her?

Oh, hell no! Mikey grinned. She's got her sources. Also, she wants in next year.

A girl snatching? Darius said as he took the note off my knee.

Yeaaaah, Mikey muttered.

I wasn't sure if he meant yes-girls or no-girls. Decided to cut him off at the pass. I said, I don't think there's going to be a next year.

Mikey's eyes narrowed, but Darius spoke first.

This isn't kid stuff. He held up the note. This is like . . . a felony. It's illegal to go 'round threatening people. I think we should tell a teacher.

Nobody's telling anything, Mikey snapped. It ain't *that* big a deal! We handle it ourselves.

Yeah, I thought. Mikey would get busted worse than Double D and me. He was the only kid we knew personally who'd gotten suspended from NR K–8. It was a million years ago in third grade, but demerits stay on your record. If school booted him, his sister would go ballistic. As it was, she had to drive Mikey's brother to some special high school an hour away because dude can't act right.

Maybe she's just trying to spook you, Darius added.

Mmm, I said, but before I could say anything else, Stew called for me from up front.

As we stood, Mikey said, We got your back.

Did he?

*   *   *

As the boys filed out, I helped Stew haul boxes for the Patrick & Moore order to a double-parked SUV. Lugging the rickety hand-cart back up on the curb, I listened to Stew chat up the driver and pulled in a deep breath: cold, wet salt air wafting from the marina, car exhaust, and pine smell from the holiday planters dotting the sidewalk. Took another breath and looked up at the street lanterns lighting the red cobblestones. It felt good to be quiet.

Breath blowing out like a whale come up for air, Stew stepped beside me and rolled down the sleeves of his flannel shirt.

He said, Christmas is in about a month, and I'm behind on our holiday display. Lucky your mom hasn't said anything yet.

When he wasn't too busy with college, Stew designed Soho's window displays. My sister, who's been silly about Stew pretty much since she learned to talk, throws a fit if she doesn't get to help. I keep explaining to her: you're seven, he's twenty. That's just wrong. Plus he's into dudes, but Rex ain't having it. And whenever Mom catches me, she scolds: Leave her be, Baby Bear. Roxanne's not hurting anybody.

I'd pulled out my phone to set a reminder to tell my sister about the displays when I heard a voice say, Yeah, it's great when y'all put up those cute little snowmen because then people see our display at North River Books and are REALLY impressed.

Stew fake-gasped, putting a hand to his heart. He said, Your words cut like ICE, McCormick.

Robin, who is Stew's age and manages the bookstore down the way, stopped beside us. She toasted me with a steaming cup and took a good look at our windows. Her jacket—jean with a giant white woolly collar, long ribbons attached to the back that hung nearly to her ankles—couldn't be warm, but it sure was interesting.

Charity O'Dell, take a lesson, I thought.

I vote you add an abominable snowman this year, said Robin as she scratched her spiky dark hair.

Sabotage, Stew said, taking Robin's shoulder and spinning her in my direction. Let me distract you by introducing my good friend Jonas Abraham. You may think you already know him, but you don't. This is the NEW Jonas.

Robin, playing along, pumped my hand forcefully. Oh, yeah? Nice to meet you. What's NEW?

Stew spoke before I could. He's a budding zinester! He's publishing one with his friend, Single Initial. But wait, there's MORE. Last week, he got a typewriter of. His. Very. Own. Amazing, right?

Robin: Yeah? (hand in front of her mouth, loud-whispering) Ko here tried to foist that thing on me. I told him, ah-ah.

Stew: I'm offended.

Robin (loudly sipping): How's it going for you? Doing lots of inspired typing?

Me (picturing the hideous pink typewriter, making a face):

Stew (plucking cup from Robin's hand and taking a giant gulp): As you can see, Jonas here is a man of many words. Unfortunately, he writes most of them on paper, so when it comes time to speak . . . well, you see what happens.

I laughed as Robin leaped to snatch back her drink, Stew holding it way up high.

I'm not really the one making the zine, I explained as Robin did some kinda ballet beside me and the color strips hanging from her jacket fluttered like streamers.

As an afterthought, I added, I'm helping.

Robin said, Either way, come by North River Books. We keep zines in stock. I'll hook you up.

Me (wrapping my arms around myself, stamping my feet): Yeah?

Robin (hot drink retrieved and backing away toward her store, out of Stew's reach): We have a big collection—good, local stuff.

Stew (swinging arms zombie-like): Cooooffee!

Robin: Bring your friend. There might be free access to a copy machine for zine makin'. But you didn't hear that from me.

Back in Soho Stationery, I folded the handcart, stashed it where it belonged, and glanced at my phone. Mom would be by soon to pick me up.

Hey, little man. Stew woke me from my thoughts, leaning back on his elbows against the counter. Something happen earlier with you and your buddies?

I just looked at him, surprised.

Sounded a little tense, he added.

Everything's fine, I said, and ducked down to retie my sneaker . . . maybe hide my face.

Stew waited for me to finish and stand. He looked at me for a long moment and then nodded like I'd explained something. Long strands of red hair came loose from behind his ears and swung like a curtain around his face. And you'd tell your old buddy Stew if something was off, right?

God. I really hoped he hadn't heard Mikey's big mouth. In my face, heat throbbed that I hadn't felt even when Mikey was blabbing on. Earlier, it was more important to put a lid on him, but now? Now it made me crazy that one of my best boys had acted so ignorant. My parents, Nana, nobody I knew would ever treat Stew bad or talk crap about him. Back when he babysat us, Stew used to carry Rex in one of those chest slings. This winter, his guyfriend Anthony promised to teach me to snowboard, and in general, he was mad cool.

Sometimes I just didn't get people.

Stew held up the square of paper and said, I found this. Your name's on it.

I didn't take the paper. No need. I knew what it said: TELL. OR I WILL.

Play it off, I told myself. Stew finding out about Halloween wouldn't be good. The candy snatching I couldn't see him caring much about, but what happened with Gideon? Yeah. Bad.

The part of me that used to squish on the love seat with Stewart and toddling Rex, eatin' popcorn and readin' through a fat stack of picture books—that Jonas . . . that Jonas might say, Stew, I think I'm in trouble. There's something going on at school.

But this Jonas, secret-wolf Jonas, the Jonas who hit the ground same time as that girl, who was swallowed up by silence until the struggling got loud. Until gasping. Until rolling. Until fists. Pain.

THIS Jonas said, Throw it out. It's a joke.

*　*　*

C'mon, Jonas, Rex demanded. Teach me!

Rex was doing her Ramona thing, like the teddy-bear-assaulting kid in those books Stew used to read us back when he babysat. After homework, dinner, and about fifty rounds of Candy Land, I'd had enough. It was Jonas Time.

I lay on my bed with Mom's phone that I'd ferreted away after she disappeared to the den to read work emails. I was one board away from winning the dragon-fruit level on Veggie Pirate Revenge and figured I could finish before Mom noticed.

Go away, I said without looking up from the game.

My sister rolled the desk chair backward, toes barely touching the floor. Got as far as a big pile of clothes in the middle of the room before abandoning ship and advancing on my bed. She swung her arms like they do in the Olympics, twisted midair, and landed butt-first, bouncing us both.

Jooonas. Jooonas, she whined, thumping the box spring with her heels.

Because she jostled my arm, I missed an important jump and my veggie pirate plummeted to a squishy death.

Girl! I sat up. What is *wrong* with you? Mom and I played with you for like an hour. Find something else to do.

I want to TYPE on the TYPEWRITER!

What? I said. You can barely read.

Rex stuck her tongue out at me. Rude! Mom says I learned to read earlier than *you*.

Good for you, I mumbled as I thumb-tapped to a redo.

Rex heaved a dramatic sigh, got to her feet, and shuffled in her too-long jeans back to the desk. If the typewriter had been hidden beneath piles of junk, like the rest of my bedroom, she might have forgotten about it. Hard to ignore the new toy in the house, all shiny and pinker than a tutu.

KLAAACCCCKKK!

Hey! I jumped and spotted my sister glancing over her shoulder, eyes sly, both hands pressing the keys.

Are you a girl or a cat? I grumbled as I dropped Mom's phone and struggled up off the bed.

What's this? Rex plucked a paper from the desk and read aloud. Worst thing I ever did . . .

I snatched the haiku from her grubby paws.

You wrote on the back of Dad's mail, she accused as I jammed the haiku-velope into a schoolbook.

Realizing I should move the zines out of sight, too, I started gathering stuff.

Yeah, well, I said. Dad doesn't live here. He should make his mail go to his place.

It's a poem? Rex asked, out of nowhere.

It's nothing, I said.

I'm gonna write a poem, too, Rex singsonged as she tapped her fingers across the keys, pretending.

Would you sto— I started, but then I remembered what I read in that zine: "A Recipe for Disaster—Ingredients," with the picture of a kid like my sister. Little girl smirking; those star glasses.

Rex started spinning in a circle, jabbing at the typewriter keys each time she came 'round, and I intercepted the chair with my knee. Before she opened her trap to complain, I plucked a sheet of paper from my desk and fluttered it loudly. Then, like the YouTube tutorials showed, I fed it through the machine's levers and rolls.

Standing behind Rex, stooped enough to smell her coconut and sugar, I took my kid sister's stubby fingers and held them stiff enough to poke the keys. Together we watched letters appear, black and loud and slow. The ultimate zine machine.

Hey, I said to Rex's hair as an idea bloomed. Know what?

What? Rex leaned her head back and blinked her giant eyes.

A typewriter isn't like a phone or a laptop, where you can erase. It works better if you already have something to copy from.

Really?

That's how I do it, I explained. Look, here's some homework I wrote by hand. You wanna try and type it?

Rex shook her head, looking a bit suspicious. Mmm-mm!

Okay, I said. How about writing your own story? You could tell it and I'll type for you.

She considered a moment, then scooched to make room for me. I sat with half my butt.

A story about what? Rex asked.

I pretended to think hard, then said, How about: the worst thing you ever did?

* * *

Rex went off to handwrite herself a story, and I picked up Mom's phone. Aunt Demi was madly texting about her lawyer boyfriend who she AGAIN caught checking out women's butts, *at church*. Knowing I shouldn't, I scrolled and read: Livie, you're waaaay better at choosing quality men. K. Maybe things tanked with Tru? I have faith y'all can work through it, God willing.

Makes one of us, I said aloud, swiping back to Veggie Revenge.

Next *my* phone started buzzing. Returning to my desk, I saw Darius had left a string of messages.

DD: Mikey learned where your stalker lives. He's TPing her parents' car. They have a TESLA

DD: Wish my dad would buy a Tesla

DD (forwarded photo with blurry car and a blurry house behind it):

DD (photo of somebody, maybe Mikey, crouched low):

DD: G lives in a sweet house

DD: They have a pool shaped like a paisley

Me: ??

Even though I had a phone in my hand, I checked my alarm clock out of habit.

Me: How are you not home at 9:00 on a Wednesday?

DD: I am. These are from after we left your mom's shop

DD: Only took a little Google-Fu to find G's address. Her dad really IS a big deal

Me (*kill, kill*): What's Mikey's PROBLEM?????????

DD: . . .

DD: He's a hoodlum?

Me: What is YOUR problem? You're egging him on

DD: I'm a hoodlum?

I dropped my phone to grab a handful of my own hair. The other phone buzzed.

Demi: Livie, come to Queens for Thanksgiving. I know you're not answering because you are working TOO hard. Leave the kids with him. We'll do the Korean Spa and get drunk at 230 Fifth.

Last year, even though they'd split, we all spent Thanksgiving with Nana. I vote for Aunt Demi's plan.

My phone buzzed again.

DD: Don't be mad. Not my idea!

DD: Maybe the notes will go away now

Me: Mikey tp'ed her house but SHE'LL THINK I DID IT

DD: . . .

DD: Just the car. And that might be true

DD: IDK tell him to knock it off? You know he don't listen to me! Say something at the movie marathon

Why wait that long when I can deck him tomorrow? Knock my friend on his butt, like he was knocking my rep. I frowned. Mikey was doing this on my behalf. Right? Not because he liked sneakin' around, gettin' away with stuff?

A knock on the door made me jump. It squeaked open and Mom stuck her head through.

Bear, she said. It's late. Why are you up? More importantly, why are you holding two phones?

When I opened my mouth to lie, Mom turned away to call, That better not be a flashlight I see, Roxanne! You should have been asleep half an hour ago.

I thumbed Mom's text app off. Playing games was one thing; reading private messages was another.

Sighing, she shuffled over in her fuzzy slippers.

Mom said, You run my battery down playing that vegetable game?

I started to lie again and ended up grinning. I said, Vegetable game?

Mom put a hand on her hip, then let it drop like she was too tired to bother being cross.

She huffed, You don't want to eat the healthy stuff I cook, but you steal my phone to spend hours with digital food.

Your vegetables don't level up, I informed her.

Mom rolled her eyes and wrapped her forearm 'round my head, planting a loud, smacking kiss.

I'll work on that, she said. Bed. NOW.

Chapter 6
MESSAGES

On Thursday, Charity O'Dell and me met near my sister's class-room. Upper-school kids hardly ever used the lower-level floors, so we knew it'd be a safe bet. I walked up just as Charity bent over the water fountain, holding her long hair far out of the way like she was afraid it'd nap up if it got the tiniest bit wet. More water flowed down the drain than went into her mouth. She straightened, wiping her chin. I didn't wait for her to start talking.

Double D likes Ton O' Braids okay, I reported, knowing good and well I hadn't said peep to Darius about it. What was the point? Those two were more obvious than the sun.

Nobody's seen that girl put anything in your locker, Charity replied. Homegirl don't care nothing about you.

Anyone else? I asked. Anybody you know seen someone-not-me at my locker?

What, you think my friends just stand around STARING at your locker? Charity laughed. Dang! So paranoid.

What about Mikey? I said, the words out before I could stop them.

What about him? said Charity.

I asked, He behind the notes?

Charity made a face. For why?

I told her, 'Cause he's like that, and you know it.

Charity snorted. Hah! All I know is SOME people think you're cute, so maybe you get notes from girls. But not everything is ABOUT you, and Mikey got other stuff to *do* with people in the hall.

She smiled wide over the *do*. Made me want to gag.

Keep it G-rated, I said, and then mimicked her voice. Not everything is about YOU, either. That includes Mikey.

Not true, of course; Mikey was totally about Charity. I wondered what would happen if I told her about Mikey going to another girl's house? Gideon and Mikey operated in different orbits, had no classes together since Gideon was mostly in honors, but the idea was still sure to piss Charity off. As if I needed her MORE mad . . .

Hair nearly whipped my face as Charity swept it over her shoulder and leaned forward, pointing. Don't talk about what you don't know about, Jonas Abraham, she snarled.

Maybe she would've hit me. Maybe I would've had to break her stupid finger. Neither thing happened because there was a sound behind me. Screeching of sneakers against the shined-up floor and then a body checking mine, pushing me forward into Charity, who squealed as my arms pinwheeled, connecting with some soft part of her.

Feet sped away. My ears followed the clicking and stomping as I untangled myself from Charity, but my eyes only swung around in time to catch colors. Blue and red. Two girls, and neither of them Charity's crew.

BOY! Charity hollered, shoving at me as hard as she could.

I was falling the other way, but my balance returned and I caught myself, wide-legged. Drawing a breath, I scanned the empty hall. Our bags were all that remained, pens and notebooks scattered.

Charity jumped at me, faced screwed into a rage that made her not-the-prettiest girl in seventh grade. Her hand rose to smack me, like I guess I'd socked her.

Hey! I yelled, grabbing her wrist and pushing her back with a little more force than I'd normally use on a girl. It was an accident. You saw somebody just *checked* me!

Still she came, sucking in a loud breath so she could continue shouting and score us both demerits. My hand shot over Charity's mouth so fast, surprised even myself. Her hot breath brushed my knuckles and her eyes bugged as I clapped my other hand around the back of her head and clasped her like a watermelon. A jolt went through me: last time I'd been this up and personal with a girl? *Halloween.*

Shh! I hissed in her ear before letting her go.

Ack! Gross! Charity O'Dell said, backing away and scrubbing her wrist across her mouth. I can't believe you did that!

Me neither, I thought as I wiped the wetness from her lips on my jeans.

The bell had long since rung and we could hear the lower-school kids talking loudly in their classrooms. Charity and me didn't say a word as we scrambled to pick up our things. In me, though, a word rose fast, first to my chest and then my throat.

I said, Hey, uh, sorr—

You're not! Charity accused as she rushed away.

My apology plopped flat.

* * *

Today, class, we're starting a new unit, Mrs. White said, clacking down the first row of seats in spike-heeled boots. Please! Please!

Contain yourselves. I understand that you are *explosively* excited to discover the difference between atoms and molecules.

Kids groaned. My science teacher thinks she's a real crack-up.

What is this? Mrs. White said. Complaints? Before we begin the new unit—cheers, cheers anyone? Anyway, as I was saying, before we start, I'd like a volunteer to give a sixty-second summary of the last unit on elements.

Silence. Even the rats in the tank near the windows stopped moving.

While everyone was distracted by hiding-in-place, I pulled out my book and flipped to the new unit. My phone buzzed in my pocket. We're not allowed to have phones on or out during class, so I did like every other upper-schooler and cozied it between the pages of a thick notebook on my lap.

U dont trust me, read the text when I tapped my phone on.

It was from C., who was in New York with Tío Rodrigo. Once, I mentioned how fun it sounded to get to see the different places they went for Tío's research, but according to C., she was either stuck in dry college libraries or Tío sent her to a museum with a day pass and C. wandered the exhibits till she was ready to puke.

What r u talking a/b? I typed slowly with my pointer, keeping half my sight on Mrs. White, who was squeaking across the whiteboard with a purple marker. Other kids in the class copied what she wrote, so I shoved my chair back a little to make room for writing in the notebook on my lap. A few rows over, Gideon also had a notebook on her lap. Instead of a phone, though, she hid a thick paperback book.

Got ur email u chnged ur story, said the next message.

Changed my . . . ? What was that girl talking about? Oh, the zine.

Y?

Moving my hand carefully, I scrolled twice through C.'s text. Girl hardly ever used punctuation, and sometimes it was hard deciphering what she meant, especially since she sometimes seemed to not notice or care that she was writing in another language.

Just use it, I responded.

From the next desk over, Darius watched me curiously. I shrugged one shoulder at him: it's nobody. The boys knew about C., but I always figured the less I told them the better.

Turning my attention back to class, I jotted down the reading assignment and terms while Mrs. White caught the dry-erase marker she'd tossed high over her head. (Sometimes she missed; once a kid in the front row took a marker across the forehead.)

Volunteer? Mrs. White sang. Vol-un-teeeeers?

She stopped wandering the aisles to stand in front of her big metal desk. Going once. Going twice! Gideon Rao. Thank you for volunteering.

Everybody turned in their seats. Gideon was a statue. I saw her fingers nudge the novel closed.

I . . . She slowly brought her hands out from under the desk. I . . . I was absent?

Were you? For three weeks? Mrs. White tilted her head. I seem to recall you sitting right there in your seat. Luuuucky for you, Darius has his hand raised and is going to save your bacon. Mr. Delicious?

Darius, who did have his hand up, talked about how chemical elements get together to throw parties on the periodic table of blahblahblah. In the middle of his more-than-sixty-seconds, my phone vibrated again.

¡Go bk to ur cndy stry esa historia de Roxita que lata!

I shook my head. The story about Rex is . . . something? Whatever. I didn't need to decode that to understand C. hadn't dug my newest zine submission. Why was I bothering? In about two weeks, she'd probably be distracted by a different project to SAVE THE WORLD, and my efforts would be abandoned.

Still, I liked that little poem I'd written. It wasn't much of a zine page, maybe, but sometimes it burped up while I brushed my teeth or cruised to the next level in Veggie Pirate Revenge.

Maybe send that? Part of me was like, Yeah. Thing's good-n-short. Another part of me said, Nah. It's better not to share what's real, no matter how so-called anonymous. Safer.

I texted: Get back to you on that.

Okay! shouted Mrs. White, jarring my brain. For today's lesson, she called, voice ringing over the soft shuffling of books and students whispering to each other, we're going to create our own one-act play to the tune of *Romeo and Juliet*. We'll call it, say, *Atoms Love Molecules*. Who wants in? Darius, of course. Aja, definitely. Rani, maybe . . . Jonas, *reeeaa-lly*? All right!

In one swoop I dropped my raised hand and stowed the phone in my pocket. Like Mom says, sometimes you gotta stop thinking and start moving.

*   *   *

When the bell rang, I joined the horde in the hallway. Sneakers squeaked. Two dudes yelled as they bumped, one bouncing off the wall. A hum rose from the water fountain as someone pressed the bar for a low, sparkling arch. I smelled the wet metal as I passed.

My eyes caught Gideon headed to her next class. She was alone. A kid I hadn't once spoken to bopped over, and Gideon grinned. I frowned. Who was *this* guy, his short self? I kinda wanted to stalk over and intercept with an EXCUSE ME and mush that dude's forehead. When had Gideon changed from a single shadow among many in the hallway to somebody ringed by light, who I couldn't pull my eyes from? Nerdy girl whose worst thing was probably not paying attention in class?

I knew I should get to class, but my feet had actually brought me closer to them. I sort of shook myself and started turning the ship around before they could notice me bearing down on their little bubble. Then I heard feet pounding.

I saw, Gideon saw, Short-Stocky saw Mikey charge down the hall with hands clenched and shoulders raised, and maybe we didn't want to miss who was gonna get it. The whole hallway froze, conversations shriveling and kids shrinking back, as he stomped . . . straight to me.

What were you doing with Charity? he demanded.

Wait, I thought. What?

I said, Uh?

You heard me!

I had nothing to say because what the heck? Mikey leaned in, nostrils flared.

You and her were in the hall today, by yourselves, Mikey said. Boy, you need to step off!

Hey, someone else said. Stop—

Mikey and I glanced around. Next I knew Mikey stiff-armed Short-Stocky and sent the kid stumbling, arms pinwheeling. I heard a squeak, which was maybe Gideon trying to keep her buddy from rattling on the ground like a pile of dropped pencils.

First, I thought: Who's that schmo think HE is, challenging Mikey?

Second: What does MIKEY think he's doing? I don't like Charity!

And next the bell rang. Next the hallway burst into motion, sneaker toes screeching as kids scattered. Mikey pivoted to end-zone high-step into a room two doors down.

Only putz left behind was me. A shock zinged up my spine as VP boomed: Jonas Abraham, where are you SUPPOSED to be?

* * *

I slid my third yellow slip (aka Congrats: You've Achieved Detention) between the pages of my notebook. We were starting a group exercise in language arts and kids pushed desks into pods of four. Laughing, talking, dropping stuff on the floor, yet what I saw in my head was Mikey running up on me.

What was that? Mikey and me were friends first! What's the big deal about Charity?

My legs tangled with the legs of the desk I carried and I staggered, dropping it where teacher pointed. Ton O' Braids, head pulled to the right like usual, followed. She wiggled her desk forward so ours touched. The way she was blinking, I knew she had something on me. Texting with D, likely.

Ton: I heard what happened in the hall.

Me (clouds gathering): So did everybody with ears.

Two classmates joined our pod to make four unlucky kids about to embark on the new poetry unit. I fully expected one person in this group to fly through while the others dragged loudly behind like cans tied to a cat.

Ton: I thought you and Mikey were like . . . (crosses fingers) but he sounds pret-ty mad.

Me (clouds darkening): You have someone else's business to mind?

Ton: Is this about the notes in your locker? I mean, doesn't seem Gideon would do that.

Me (thunder): Charity O'Dell's been runnin' her mouth?

Ton: Nobody said anything about Charity.

Teacher began instructions for the assignment, which thankfully made Ton hit pause. I half listened.

As our pod got situated, Ton snapped back on track. She said, I'll take blank verse if Jonas lists the structural elements of couplets. You and you: sonnet and epic? Great. Also, why would Gideon like YOU? I saw you hit her with that ball and then not apologize.

Me (lightning bolts):

Ton: What? Don't be pissed at *me*. People are sayin'—

Me: People need to stop talking.

Teacher (calling across the room): Great advice, Jonas! Take it.

I shut up. Near the end of class, something pinged in my brain and I muttered, Mikey's probably trying to throw me off the trail.

Probably, agreed Ton.

C: Nothing I write could
ever be this good. Rex typed
it herself. My title suggestion:
PRINCESS WINS!!!!
If you ask, bet she'll draw
some pictures to go with. —J

THE PRINCESS AND THE MAGIC GLASSES

By Roxanne

Once upon a time, there was a Mommy, a Daddy, a brother, and
a Princess. They were very Sad. They fought All The Time.
It was like maybe a year and then something happened. The
Daddy moved away. He didn't go too far. The brother and the
Princess now had TWO houses with woods between and that was
okay until ONE DAY the Princess and the brother saw a new
path in the woods and they followed it. The brother had a
giant cookie and he ripped it into teeny-tiny bits and made
a trail so they would NOT get lost. Then the Big Bad Wolf
came. He was working for a Witch. She didn't pay good, but
it was the only job there was. The Wolf ATE the cookie bits.
The brother and Princess couldn't find their way home. They
were so so so so so so so so so so SAD. And scared. But the
Princess was smart and she made a plan. She tiptoed into the
kitchen and got a stool and found some glasses hidden way up
high. These were very Special glasses only used for holidays
and they Glittered. Special is another way to say Unusual
and also means MAGIC. The Princess knew that she needed a
lot of MAGIC to chase away the Big Bad Wolf and his boss
the Witch. Well, the Princess was five years old but she was
STRONG. She BROKE EVERY GLASS and some plates. The MAGIC
flew up in the air and she gathered it into a great big ball
and threw the ball at the Wolf and the Witch who got caught
up in it and rolled and rolled and rolled away. The other
MAGIC thing that happened was Mommy and Daddy saw the
broken glasses and lost their voices kind of like the Little
Mermaid. The Princess was in trouble but it's okay because
in the end Mommy and Daddy started talking to each other
again. Mommy and Daddy sent the Princess and the brother
through the woods to Nana's where they ate all the pie they
wanted and watched 20 hours of Netflix.

                        THE END.

Chapter 7
HOME BASE

Lucky for me, school likes to hold upper-school students hostage on Friday afternoons. In my family, Fridays are Jonas Time—no watching Rex or finishing homework, no working a shift at Mom's shop. Having to stay behind at school when I could be playing video games with Mikey and Darius, or skateboarding with Aaron and his friends, is lame, but I'd rather that than have my parents find out.

After a conversation with VP about how I could "better embody NR K–8's school value, responsibility" (VP's words) by arriving to class promptly (my suggestion), I got to choose: sit-n-rot in detention or school community service. At three p.m., my butt belonged to Mrs. White.

Look at you, teacher said as I dropped my backpack and jacket on a desk. Sleeves rolled and ready to go!

My science teacher is big on manual labor. I know because I've walked past her room at the end of the day and seen kids bent over, cleaning and organizing, or exercising the rats. Already it looked real hard-knock up here, with five other community service "volunteers" scrubbing or whatever.

I walked over to Mrs. White's giant desk to get my assignment. A laptop sitting on a paper stack played a song I recognized from C.'s playlists. One girls like to dance along to, shimmying their hips fast like maracas.

Mrs. White checked her watch and said, I'm gonna take off my Community Service Monitor hat for a sec and put on my Honors Science hat. You ready?

I blinked. Lady wasn't wearing a hat.

Okay, Jonas, as your teacher, I believe you owe me a confession.

My stomach pitched into a gully. I stepped back. Holy crap.

The laptop started to slip off the paper pile and Mrs. White had to catch it, and then some other kids dragged themselves in, so I had a solid minute to sink into a panic and then rise back out. *Get a grip, J! What could she have on you? Too used to being IN it for something.*

Jonas, Mrs. White said, fluttering a piece of paper in my face. Earth to Jonas.

Yo, I said. Mrs. White, I added awkwardly before Mind-Mama cuffed me.

When I saw this, I couldn't believe my eyes! Mrs. White handed over what looked like a completed science assignment.

I need you to tell me, Mrs. White said.

Tell you, I parroted.

Teacher wanted me to confess. About? Biting my lip, I struggled to find something to say till I was saved by three stragglers in the doorway. Mrs. White held up a finger for me to wait and went to assign tasks.

Mrs. White returned, shaking her head, saying, I can't believe you, Jonas. Keeping this a secret.

Watching her, silver earrings swinging, yellow hair in a messy bun, I considered confessing to Mrs. White about the weirdness. Students at NR could ask a favorite teacher to step in, help talk with another student or even a teacher. Mrs. White did like me, after all. I get decent grades since, without Mikey in class to egg me on, I'm not as much of a crack-up.

Oops, Mrs. White said. Wait, whose paper do you have?

I glanced down. *Darius Delicious. A.*

Wrong one, she said, yanking the paper away. God, I am so disorganized sometimes.

This is your chance, J, I told myself. Ask! Say, Mrs. White, would you . . . can we . . . I have this . . . ? How to explain? What if she said: Jonas, manage your own problems?

Here we go! Mrs. W. handed over a rumpled sheet.

As I reached for it, my chest felt funny. Did that mean I should talk about Mikey, about Gideon and Halloween, or not? My mom says follow your intuition. Half the time, I'm like: Where's it goin'?

Glancing down, I read, in purple pen across the top of my observations journal: *A-. Good. Explain more about electrons. Also—use spell-check.*

There's an unusual number of spelling errors here, even for you. Mrs. White crossed her arms and tapped her purple painted nails. But that's not what this little conference is about. Tell me about the new typing service you've hired.

I said, What? I, uh, have a typewriter? Mom won't let me use the laptop late at night.

I glanced up. Mrs. White's expression was like when one of Aaron's skater buddies kick-flips off a bench but doesn't bomb over the railing into the river at Marine Park. She fixed her eyes on the back of the room, lifted her palm, and waited for me to figure it out.

Eventually, I got it. I slapped her five.

* * *

When I twisted my key in the door at Dad's place, the short click sounded like *SAFE!*

Million things I could usually think to do on a late Friday afternoon—video games at D's; shoot hoops with Mikey at the one park that keeps lights on past dark; surprise Rex at the Y to watch her do what she calls swimming and I call the doggy paddle, then walk her downtown for a cookie; pop in to bug C. None of it appealed.

Trying to decide whether I regretted watching Mrs. White geek out about typewriters instead of asking for help made my brain tired. The promise of a snack and a few moments of quiet had me hoofing to the one place where that could happen till at least seven, when Dad got home from work.

Kitchen light in Dad's condo shone yellow; my parents always want their houses to look like someone's home. I pictured myself planted in the beanbag chair in the living room, chillin' with a cup of Sleepytime to settle. Yeah. That sounded great.

Icy wind whipped up from the river, zigzagged through the complex, and sliced through my jacket as I stepped into the tiny foyer. In the mirror over the little bench Dad set out for shoe changing, my face was in shadow, eyes a flash of white. My color's not as deep as Darius's, but I could be one spooky dude if I wanted. If I didn't wanna, just Dad's son. Like he spit you out, Nana likes to tease. Same eyes, same little ears, same long fingers with thin nails that get brittle when it's cold.

I kicked off my sneakers. Flipped the switch beside the mirror. I was halfway up the stairs before I heard it. Scrambling.

Whoa. My heart started up. Now what?

Too big a sound to be something small and furry. Window left open? Boogeyman? Burglar after my dad's nothing (ain't got much worth stealing)?

Frozen where I was, I called, Hello?

The scrambling got louder. And then . . . swearing. I backed down a step, glanced at my sneakers in the foyer. How fast could I get them on again? Pretty fast.

I heard, whispered: What do we do?

A man cleared his throat. His first word was a squeak; the second was choked: Jonas? That you? Can you wait a sec, okay? I'll tell you when to come up. Sorry, just a . . .

A wash of relief flooded my chest. The flood kept traveling down and then it left my body entirely as I realized, standing with feet on two different steps, that Dad was up there with someone. A woman.

Who's there? I called, too shocked to not say anything.

Immediately, they stopped being quiet. I heard what sounded like people putting their full, loud weight on the floor, furniture scraping. More whispering and rushing.

I wondered, How many people are up there?

Worse, I wondered, Is one of them Mom?

I tried to decide which was a bigger horror. Mom or not-Mom? Rex and I by accident met a lady Dad was "just talking to" once. My sister was an angel the whole ten minutes, but after? Not good. For a month? Worse.

My feet started taking me up the steps. Quiet like being out in Fright Night gear with the boys. I didn't want to, but there wasn't any choice. I had a sister to take care of.

Oookay—Dad's voice sounded muffled—one second more . . .

Too late. I was already at the top, staring into the living room at my parents standing in their socks. Mom's shirt wasn't buttoned all the way. She whipped around. Even with her back to me, I could tell her hands were flying.

Jonas! she said over her shoulder. Didn't we tell you to wait?

Jonas, Dad said, taking a step toward me and tripping over the beanbag chair, which wasn't where it usually sat.

So. My parents. On a Friday, while I toiled in community service and Rex pretended to be a clown fish. I tried to resist, but my eyes dropped to Dad's slacks. Stylish and gray and not completely, not totally zipped.

This was worse than I could have imagined. I thought the floor was going to rise up and sucker punch me. It didn't. Only thing that happened is both my parents looked scared and Dad rushed toward me and Mom said, Sit down before you— and I snatched my arm out of Dad's grip, stumbling backward toward the steps.

Mom put a hand up, said, We'd better talk. Right now—let's talk.

Then she used that hand to pat down her hair. She was looking at Dad, not at me, so I looked at him, too.

I said, stupidly, Who's at the pool making sure Rex doesn't drown?

Mom said, She's in class, Baby Bear. There's an instructor.

Quickly, I lowered my eyes to the floor because I didn't want either of them to do that thing where, with just their minds, they forced me to obey. Some parent magic. Not tonight.

I'm going home, I informed them. I mean . . . the other one.

Jonas, wait, Dad said, reaching to take my arm again.

I bolted. My knees shook the whole way down to the front door. As I guessed, took just a few seconds to jam on both sneakers. I knew, once I hit the sidewalk, Dad wouldn't chase me. He doesn't like a scene.

In a way, it felt good that I was faster than my dad. The pale concrete blurred under me as I ran. I thought I heard Mom shout, but maybe that was the wind.

* * *

C. opened her door wearing her rabbits-with-fangs slippers, and Tío Rodrigo sat at the kitchen table going through a stack of books. Big pile of boring in bright primary colors.

¿Como estás, Jonasito? Tío called as I came in and toed off my kicks. ¿Café?

I shook my head no as C., drinking coffee at six p.m. like her uncle, asked, How'd you know we're back from New York?

Didn't, I said as I trailed her through their small bungalow. Aside from the screened porch, we spent most of our time in the kitchen. The rest of the house was practically empty, compared to my two houses. I guess because they spent so much time away. C.'s room though . . . C.'s room was like being inside a kaleidoscope: bright shapes and colors. Tattered cloth flags from Tibet stretched across the window, clashing with her ten-color comforter loaded with tiny, glittery disks shining like mirrors. On top of that, triangle pillows with frizzy tassels that Cuidado likes to attack, white-tipped black tail swinging.

I flopped facedown on the bed, and the cat jumped up to pad across my back. On his way to Tassel Attack, the Sequel.

I'm going to have to move in, I told C.

Yeah? she said, sipping.

I said, You got room, right?

Oh, sí poh, she said. You'll take care of Cuidado when Tío and me are traveling, instead of my homeschool friend. She feeds him too much. Gato gordo—C. puffed out her cheeks—fat cat!

So many things felt wrong. And dumb. Wrong and dumb. I was drowning in how ridiculous everything felt, tipping like a raft, side to side. Oh, wait, that was C. I cracked one eye. Girl leaned directly over me, blue eyes boring down.

Ugh, I groaned.

Problema, she declared.

Maybe, I said.

I didn't know what Tío would say if he saw us close together—C. and me weren't usually allowed to be alone in her room, which was . . . ridiculous. We're not about anything 'sides homework and hanging out.

What's with you? she asked. Some tummy thing? She nudged me hard. Off my bed if you're gonna yur—

I'm good, I croaked. It's just I—I saw— I . . .

C.'s door, which was cracked open, pushed wider. The smell of peppers and spices wafted in, and then Tío's head appeared, black-and-gray curls all over. He raised his bushy eyebrows but said nothing about how we needed to be at least a foot apart or something. "Put God between us."

Jonasito. Staying for dinner? he asked.

I shrugged. Couldn't eat if I wanted right now.

He crinkled his brow. Your mamá knows you're here, no poh?

I thought, No. Shrugged again, glad my phone was off so it couldn't give me away.

It's Friday, I said, hedging. My time to do what I want.

Tío fixed me with a look I couldn't figure and said to C., Supper in twenty, Concepción.

After he disappeared, C. shook herself the way she always does when someone uses her actual name. Music started up in the kitchen, Chilean folk-rock with drums, flute, and shredding guitar.

C. poked my shoulder. Y'know . . . lot of folks don't have a mamá y papá, Jonasito. Drive niños ricos around wherever they want, sign 'em up for classes at the Nature Center.

I twitched away.

C. made one of those sounds that says nothing and bopped me on the forehead with a piece of rolled-up paper.

I flailed, startling the cat, who'd joined us to bat at my hoodie ties. Cuidado dug his claws into my shoulder before darting away. Owww! I said.

She handed me the roll.

What's this? I asked, unfurling it.

Ubícate, she said, shaking a piece of paper in my direction.

Here's a mockup of my page, she added as I took in the paper she handed me.

The words were obviously printed from a computer in a frilly font. Stew was right: typewriter looked better. More serious. More punk.

Tío reappeared.

Jonasito, he said, voice heavy like a cloud ready to hail. You don't tell the truth, no poh? Got a call here.

He hefted a tablet-size phone in my direction. Es tu mamá.

Lo Peor

by Concepción Bianca Cosmos Flores

Getting kicked out of guardería for biting a girl wasn't the
worst thing I ever did.

Falling off a roof free-running wasn't the worst thing.

There was this time I opened the door to a dude wearing blue like a
delivery guy but un repartidor wouldn't grab, claw me, silent yanking
and yanking like he did. Threw my fist forward and that man
fell back. Maybe I got lucky.

Mami saw me later scratched and shaking but alive. She said,
Revoltosa I know you don't want to leave but it's not safe. It's long
past safe.

Mabuela came over. She said, Secuestro and we can't pay. No hay
dinero. Send Concepción to her papá. What about your brother? Fly
her to the States.

Getting on that airplane, Chile to Jersey, wasn't the worst. It was
kinda like, ¡See you mañana! ¡Y mañana y más mañana . . .!

When Mabuela calls Tío Rodrigo, she says, Put her on.

Crackly voice. Between us a hundred mañanas.

Mabuela says, Be a good girl, niña! No pongas a tú mamá en peligro.
Es solo un año.

I'm not a good girl. I bite babies. I jump roofs. I fight weones who
want to drag me and kill me dead because of what Mamita writes.
I live six thousand miles from una mamita, mi única abuela. Who
CARES if I'm good?

Mabuela says, Don't make your mamá worry.

   It's okay for me to worry?

      Tío tells me, Put Chile out of your head for now.
        Be patient.

         But sometimes he clicks his teeth, taps my
            chin with his knuckle, and says,
               You know what? No importa.
               Yo entiendo. You're just a kid.

                  Eso es lo peor.

Chapter 8

FOLLOWED

The moment Mom and Rex walked in from yoga, Mom hit me with Let's Talk eye rays and I deflected. Nope. NONE of that. Before Mom started setting out lunch, I spoke the Magic Words in front of Rex and the kid piped up with, I wanna goooo. Grabbed her hand and hit the pavement.

Fifteen minutes of her short, scuffing stride, and we came in view of downtown North River. I figured kid was due a treat since I lured her out of the house. Instead of the proper lunch Mom probably expected me to buy at Mr. Pizza, I steered my sister into No Ordinary's for chocolate chip cookies the size of salad plates.

We picked our way through dudes with glasses on laptops and high school gossip girls and tired, shopping aunts. Rex flopped in a stained armchair as I went to the counter and got us some treats. With my palm open for the change, I caught sight of familiar faces on the street. Noooo? Yes. Gideon and two girls. My heart did a thing and I told it, Settle down. Big ole sheet of glass between me and them; also they'd need to cross the street to spot me.

They crossed. One of the girls I didn't really know. She glanced at the coffee shop but no way she saw me, or cared. I could be any seventh grader holding a cookie bigger than his face, standing near a little girl with her hair in two giant puffs. Was I worried? Nah. I could take Gideon; Halloween proved that. As for those other girls, they were . . . tall, sure.

Rex scooted back in her seat so her legs stuck out. She said, Oh. Those are the girls been followin' us.

I stared as Rex took a cartoon-mouse-size nibble of her cookie.

I said, What?

I asked, When? TODAY?

Kid and I looked through the window and Gideon had gotten closer. She wasn't looking in our direction but one of those other girls was. She had thick legs and was wide up top, with shoulders good for leaning in and shoving. Was she the one tried to put me through the locker? The girl pointed.

Thinking fast, I flipped around and stood in front of Rex with my back to the window.

A little bit today, Rex said. But I've also seen them before.

They still walking this way? I asked Rex.

Few doors down, she replied, and nibbled with her eyes a little crossed.

She said, Who are they? Is one of them your girlfriend?

No! I said.

My heart said, *Thumpathumpa.*

She said, I thought she was, the one with the braid.

I thought, WHAT?

Before I could respond, Rex's eyes widened and she popped up out of her seat. She pulled my sleeve. I need to use the bathroom.

I trailed my sister to the counter. I'm about to ask for the key (a giant whisk that Rex like to stir the air with). Instead of waiting, Rex continued down the narrow hall.

Hey! I said, but she didn't turn and went right on past the bathroom.

By the time I caught up, Rex was past the mops, boxes, and an abandoned typewriter lying on its side. (Is there one in every shop storeroom?) We cleared No Ordinary's rear door and slipped into the alley, where the chill air wrapped around us.

My sister said, Safe!

My kicks hit the pebbly pavement of the back alley where the workers kept their cars. We stood for a moment. Sky was dry and everything smelled like metal and oil and dirt.

I said, From?

Rex bit her cookie and grinned.

Never mind, I said. You're getting sneaky in your old age.

I pictured Rex in an all-black outfit, crouching behind a bush on Halloween. My grin turned grimace, though, when the real Rex decked out in this year's handmade double-helix costume appeared in my imagination: screaming as middle-school dudes, dressed dark-n-scary, ran her down.

Suddenly I didn't want my cookie. Glared at the thing like it was frontin' until I heard Rex saying my name.

Let's go see Robin, my sister said, waving from the far end of the parking lot (how had she gotten that far without my noticing?). And then Stewart, like you promised!

Slipping the cookie into my pocket, I caught up to Rex and pulled open the heavy rear door of North River Books. My sister bopped through, munching her cookie into a crumbling half-moon. I gave the parking lot a quick once-over and, thankfully, no bruisers appeared to check me into next week. Maybe they hadn't even been heading to No Ordinary's, but still I was glad for Rex's quick thinking.

Like she said: safe.

* * *

How do you know which way to go? I asked, trailing my kid sister through another narrow hall, passing an overflowing stockroom and an equally stuffed office.

Rex smiled mysteriously and wrapped up the rest of her cookie in plastic to save for later. Nobody seemed shocked by a small girl shooting out of nowhere through the tall, dark stacks. I, of course, scored suspicious side-eyes, one old guy turning his head like an owl to keep me in his sight like I'd mug him while he read about the Civil War.

North River Books is three times the size of Soho Stationery, so took me a few minutes more to pick my way around the display tables, calendar racks, greeting cards, and piles of tempting toys for book nuts. I passed the kids' section, with its super-low tables and tiny wooden chairs; paused by the game guides to see if there were any manuals for the fighting game Darius had promised to trade me; and finally arrived at checkout, a long wooden counter raised up off the floor like a throne. Rex had already exploded a talk-bomb, so Robin waggled two fingers at me as she leaned her chin on her crossed hands and smiled through my sister's deluge.

These girls were gonna GET Jonas so I said QUICK! And one girl, she has black hair like—my sister drew two lines from her giant fore-head to her waist (exaggeration)—and when she turns her head it goes

WHOOSH, it didn't do that today because she had a braid, don't tell my brother, but one time? I saw her looking in the window at our store—Rex cupped her own face with both hands—she's really pretty, know what I think? She *likes* Jonas and THAT'S why she—

I put more pep in my step and dropped a hand over the pest's mouth. She licked me, which I knew she would. Whole tongue on my palm. Nasty.

Rex danced out of reach as I wiped my hand on my pants.

Wow, Robin said, smiling and tugging the largest of the six gold rings climbing up her ear. Your sister has the scoop of the century. Roxi, please don't stand on that ledge.

Sorry, said Rex as she jumped, sneakers kicking against the wood, down from where she'd clambered to spy what was on top of the counter.

All untrue, I told Robin.

Rex loud-whispered, He's embarrassed.

Robin laughed, straightening up, and I saw that her T-shirt read, in teeny-tiny letters: IF YOU CAN READ THIS, COME CLOSER AND I'LL SHOW YOU MY FISTS.

Which made me feel weird because I *could* read it. Then I had to come up with a reason for staring, so I said, My friend C. would love that shirt.

Limited edition, said Robin. She plucked at it, adding, I screen-print 'em. You wanna buy?

I said, You, too? C.'s been going on about screen-printing covers for the zine. We'll see.

Got your doubts, huh? Robin said. This is the project Stewart mentioned, right?

I shrugged. It's going nowhere fast . . . plus she travels all the time and doesn't go to regular school.

STOP TALKING, I told myself. Why are you telling her all this?

Robin's eyebrow drifted up. She said, Doesn't go to school?

She does homeschool, Rex supplied while conveniently forgetting about not climbing.

Rex added, Jonas goes to her house and actually does homework. I've seen it.

What do you mean, actually? I said. I ALWAYS do my homework. More than you can say, and you're only in second grade!

More and more interesting. Robin smiled and then said, Roxi, get down. Everybody pause; I need to take this customer.

I grabbed my sister and dragged her back as Mr. Suspicious bought a magazine and some greeting cards instead of the Civil War book that he'd probably half finished. Through the double front doors, I saw that the sidewalk was stuffed with shoppers but empty of seventh-grade girls. Time to jet.

I nudged Rex. Before I said the Magic Words (Let's visit Stew!), Robin called out, HOLD.

She said something to another worker, who took her place, then came around to us.

You gonna bring your friend to visit? Robin asked. Like I said, we have a solid zine section.

I shrugged.

Rex said, My brother doesn't like to be seen with girls.

I pushed her with my elbow, said, What are YOU, then?

Your sister. Rex rolled her eyes.

One more time and they'll stick, I warned her. Promise.

Robin interrupted with a thin stack of papers. She said, Here. Give these to your friend.

What is it? I asked.

Inspiration, Robin said. On the house.

I tried to hand them back respectfully. I said, That's okay. I'm not into this zine thing, anyway.

Robin denied me, palm up. She lip-farted. Who said they're for you?

* * *

Sunshine. Rainbows. Ponies. Rex was the HAPPIEST KID EVER.

I watched her babbling away at Stew and Anthony while they stood on different-height stepladders, leaning toward each other. You'd think jealousy would jam her trap, but nope. Ant's tattooed biceps bulged as he pinned parts of the new display to the ceiling, and when Rex turned to get something, he leaned across the distance and planted one on Stew's lips.

How can she not notice? I wondered, slowly shaking my head.

I plunked myself in the wedding nook, where I half flipped through Robin's zines (pretty strange), half texted about the movie marathon Darius had proposed. To me, he'd said we needed hangin' and bondin' time. Who knows how he sold it to Mikey? Aaron was easier and usually game to hang.

Darius: Hows 11?

Mikey: Morning or nite

Darius: Afternoon

Aaron: morning? yawl can count me out

Darius: 1 then

The front door opened and a few older teens came in. No one I knew, so I went back to my convo. Off the clock, I only planned to stay at Soho long enough to satisfy the bargain for Rex letting me drag her downtown to avoid Mom. Once kid got her fill, we would hit up Mr. Pizza before she broke or melted down from too much sugar and not enough cheese.

Aaron: what we watching? everybody bring something

Mikey: D can stream, right

Darius: Plus my dad has DVDs and Blu-ray

Aaron: u got sleepless in seattle?

Mikey: Man shut up

Aaron: ;^D no for real. i ♥ chix flix

Aaron: how many we watchin?

Personally, I'd watch movies for weeks if it kept me away from home(s).

Aaron: yawl still got candy from halloween?

Mikey: Sold it or ate it

Darius: I do. Let's finish it off

Aaron: i got nada. jonas threw his in a bush, right?

Me: Dont remind me

Right, Jonas? Rex said directly into my ear, making me jump.

Jeez, Rex, I said, staring into her giant, too-close eyes. What do you want?

I can stay here with Stew and Ant because I already ate lunch, my sister said as she made her eyes even more giant and slowly nodded like she was trying to hypnotize me.

What? I said, looking past her for shock numero dos.

Mom stood at the front of the shop, chatting with the guys. Anthony had come down off the ladder and looked like a skater gnome standing next to beanpole Stewart, wide and burly and blond with his arms crossed while Stew teased my mother like the crazy-fearless dude he is. They all laughed.

Oh, no, I thought. (Though it *was* surprising my parents had let me go this long. When Mom picked me up / kidnapped me from C.'s last night, she made a lot of noise about how we were gonna have a serious sit-down. When we got in the house, though, we retreated to our separate corners. *Ding-ding!* Till round two.)

I melted in the armchair, letting my legs flop on the floor and hopefully disappearing out of sight behind the shelving. No such luck. A rainbow of half-size envelopes and cover stock couldn't save me. Bear, said Mom, coming around in her bright headwrap and weekend-casual flats.

I'm in the middle of something, I mumbled, and ran my thumb across the screen of my phone.

You're not working, clearly, she said. Or doing anything that can't be interrupted. Let's go clock some Momma and Baby Bear time; Roxanne says she's not hungry.

Could you not call me that in public? I said.

Mom tilted her head and pursed her lips, eyeing me. I was playing a dangerous game, I knew. 'Stead of telling me a thing or two, she swung her giant weekend purse so it knocked lightly against my knee.

Let's go, she said, and strolled to the door. I heard the bells clang as she opened it and called over her shoulder to the guys. You guys'll be fine for a bit, right?

We're good! I heard Stew say.

Anthony boomed, Rex'll help us get these snowmen under control! Rex squealed her victory.

And me? I thought: Traitors. All of them.

* * *

Over the *clik-clik-clik* of the blinker, Mom said, Always running my phone down playing that fruit game.

I was sitting in the car, trapped, on my way to a Serious Talk. Seemed the least she could do was give up some battery power.

Well, you won't let me have a real phone, I muttered.

North River rolled by and by: train tracks, Volvo dealership, kitchen redesign place, dentist. A light tug on my ear pulled me back.

C'mon, Bear, she said as she turned in to a parking lot. Before you get too invested and I need to pry it from your cold, dry hands.

I passed over the phone; couldn't hardly concentrate anyway. I peered through the windshield at the Rita's, where you could easily see the giant-lettered flavors list. The outside benches and picnic tables were deserted, but inside two teens stood talking. Most summery places close in October, but this Rita's hangs on till Thanksgiving.

You know it's winter? I asked, in case she wasn't clear.

Mom glanced at her smartwatch. Not according to my calendar.

Italian ice isn't a vegetable, I said.

Stay here, then, and I'll pick out a flavor for you, Mom said, opening her door and letting cold air whoosh in. I'm thinking a scoop of bubble gum topped with a scoop of dill pickle.

Obviously, I chose something normal. After we returned to the car, our Italian ice not-really-melting beneath plastic-capped cups, Mom drove to Marine Park, just down from the shopping district and Soho. We watched the wind-chopped water from inside the car with heat blasting, listened to boring R&B on the radio.

Out of the blue, Mom asked, How's your friend Concepción?

I hesitated. . . . Fine?

Mom (nodding): Hmm. With so much . . . going on, I'm glad you have someone to talk to.

Me (in my head): *Here it comes.*

Me (redirecting): Anyway, it's kind of none of your business.

Mom (stares with guava ice smeared across her mouth):

Me: Uh . . . ma'am.

Mom (head jerking back): *Ma'am?* I—you've gotten so . . . do we need to have a conversation about tone, Jonas?

Me (directing gaze to lap, where I start folding the empty lemon ice cup in on itself):

Mom:

Me (slowly shaking my head): No. I'm sorry.

Mom (sighing): What's the deal, Bear? I'm trying; you're not meeting me halfway.

Me: I don't—I don't want to talk about it.

Our eyes met and Mom didn't ask what *it* was or say *Tough*, like she might if I was in trouble over chores or school or for pestering Rex. My chest felt tight, half like my heart was squeezing down to the size of a walnut and half like something inside wanted to fly out, to snap and snarl and bite.

My mother looked about to speak, but I jerked open the door and took my empty cup to a wooden trash barrel, which for once wasn't overflowing onto the ground. Sharp air crept up under my coat as I dragged out returning. Reprised my treatment of the door, flopped in the seat, and crossed my arms.

Without waiting a beat, Mom said, We need to talk about last night—

Me (cringing): We don't.

Mom (talking right over me): I apologize. Your dad apologizes. That shouldn't have happened.

Silence, except for the pounding in my ears. My hands went hot, cold, and prickles started over my skin. Didn't want to remember or think about what I saw or listen to the voice in my head (which didn't sound like Mind-Mama or anything Dad would say) remind me how Rex was going to grow up screwy because what she wanted most was for our parents to get back together for good. For real and forever. The part of me that had stopped foolishly wishing, who knew what other kids' families looked like, expected my parents to continue this way: half on, mostly off, mad and hurt and endlessly explaining how it wasn't Rex's or my fault, as if that made things okay.

Taste on my tongue was bitter instead of sweet like the lemon ice I'd eaten as I said, Those are just words.

Mom: Jonas—

She stopped, sighing while stuffing her empty Italian ice container into the cup holder. She folded her hands together and stared out the window with the car's hot air venting at our faces.

Me:

Mom:

Sun (outside the windshield, starting to set in strips of blue, gray, and grayish blue):

Mom: I don't know what to tell you, Jonas, that will make things better. You don't have to accept our apologies, but we . . . *I* can't do magic. I know you and Rex think Dad and I have the answers because we're the adults. I wish.

Me: But you do! You could just . . . stop.

Mom (squinting): Jonas, what are you saying?

I pressed my lips together and forced the words down down down. Ran my fingers across the door latch.

Mom: Because it's *not* your place to pass judgment or tell *adults*—

Door (snap of the latch, swings partway open):

Wind (fills the car with river smell):

Mom (reaching for me): Wait. No, you don't! Once is enough for this kind of behav— Where do you think you're going?

I dodge her and slip outside. The moment my kicks touch down, crunching leaves and gravel, my chest loosens. I can breathe.

Me: I don't want to talk anymore. I'm heading back to Soho.

Mom (leaning across the seats, looking up at me): Get in the car, Jonas. It's cold out. It's winter.

Me: You said it wasn't. I'll walk. It's ten minutes.

Mom: You will *not* walk away from me!

But I've had enough, and my feet tell me to *go*, so I do and, strangely, Mom lets me.

Sun (dim, fades):

C: You said the zine is anonymous but triple-promise you won't tell? No news reporters (like your MOTHER).

—JA

WHY I SHOULD BE DRAFTED FOR THE NFL

My best candy-snatching experience happened in sixth grade.

Me and my boys hid in a park on a dead-end street while Darius mooned a house. I almost busted a gut watching him yank his pants up and run away, getting out of sight before the front door opened. When he reached us, Aaron and Mikey cheered—nice one, high-five!

I spotted something more interesting. A group of trick-or-treaters, some our age and some younger. Bunch of girls yakking as they cut through the park. Bad idea.

WHOOP! WHOOP! When they saw us, they took off in a clump like a herd of elephants on the Nature Channel, thundering and breaking down trees. Except lil' kids can't truck. Me and my boys blew over them like smoke. Somebody's bag ripped and scattered candy on the pavement—pappappappap!

I grabbed a girl with a sack heavy enough to give somebody a concussion. She was slippery! Pulled away and tried to fake me out running in the opposite direction. I howled laughing. First, I let her think she'd swept me. Then, like a tight end, I leaped and grabbed her, midair. The witch folded like a pillow. I twisted to hit the ground first when we landed.

Football scout would've signed me then and there. Forget high school, college—straight to the NFL!

Tossing her candy sack over my shoulder, I saw the lil' witch press mitten-gloves over her eyes, shaking like a wrinkled brown leaf.

Somebody shouted COME ON! I grabbed the girl, set her standing, and tilted her pointy hat before I left.

Chapter 9
POPE IN THE WOODS

Does the pope fall in the woods? Mikey lisped.

I glanced to see why he sounded funny and spotted two Twizzlers dangling from his mouth like floppy red tusks. Shook my head. Mikey was parked on the huge white leather sofa that split the Deliciouses' den in two sections, one side with a roll-up movie screen and shelves of DVDs and video games, the other end containing a foosball table and the squat Ms. Pac-Man arcade game that Mr. Delicious had renovated as a side project.

Place was playland, though I wasn't feeling all that playful. I was on Day 2 of Operation Don't Go Home. Day 1 concluded with Stew dropping Rex and me home after Disaster Dessert with Mom. I said I wasn't feeling good and hid in my room, then snuck down at midnight and devoured me some pickles and microwave popcorn. Sunday morning I pushed for an early start to the movie marathon we hadn't exactly agreed on. I wasn't much in the mood to deal with Mikey, but you bet I told Mom that we'd been planning it for

MONTHS, how did she not remember, I said it so many times and of course my Sunday plans included homework, which I'd do later at Dad's, okay? Thanks. Out.

That's not how the saying goes, Darius snorted as he nearly backed into me, turning from the tall wall cabinets to the right of the movie screen with an armload of DVDs.

Two DVD cases hit the rug, and I scooped them up to hand to him before making my way to the foosball table, where we'd balanced snacks on the heads of the players, even though Mr. Delicious tells us not to do that.

I gotta split at six, I told the boys while digging through a pillow-case of loose candy left from Halloween.

There was more than I'd expected. I hadn't gotten much myself this year, only what Rex and Dad had brought home. I inspected the drinks balanced on the corners: Coke, 7 Up, and that fruity, spar-kly, healthy-lookin' seltzer that D's mom pushes.

I asked Darius, How many movies you think we can watch before then?

I don't know, Darius said as he spread plastic cases across the couch. Three?

Nearby, Ms. Pac-Man ran its start screen. I paused to watch Blinky, Inky, Pinky, and Sue ghost around. It was kind of meditative.

Darius's phone chirped, and Mikey bounced up off the couch to pluck it from the usual storage spot, hidden in his sweatshirt hood.

It's Aaron, Mikey said, thumbs poised and ready. He slurped a little and swung his Twiz-tusks. Vat shoo I tell hem?

Lost as usual? I asked, jamming some Junior Mints into my mouth. I reached to take the phone from Mikey, but he jerked it away and wandered across the room.

Do popes pee in the woods? he said. I called it: Aaron couldn't get here without somebody holdin' his hand.

That's definitely not the saying! Darius laughed. And there's only one pope. He lives in Vatican City, not the woods, and when there's a new pope, he gets elected by magic smoke.

Nobody cares, Mikey said.

Are you even gonna send him the address? I watched him duck-walk away. Or are you just gonna mess with him?

Mikey finished his walrus impression and started speed-sucking Twizzlers into his mouth, both at the same time. Loud and gross.

Fine, D-Brain, he said, thumbs tapping. How's the sayin' go, then?

Does a tree fall in the woods? Darius tried and stopped, scratching his head with the corner of a DVD case.

When Mikey passed the foosball for the second time, I intercepted and grabbed D's phone, ignoring Mikey's HEEEY.

This isn't his address, I said, frowning at the nonsense he'd been typing. That's, like, three doors down. Just walk right in, we're downstairs? What are you telling him?

Mikey cracked up, and Darius said, Hasn't he been here before?

You're such a menace, Dennis, I informed Mikey as I redirected Aaron.

But I was smiling a little.

To hide it, I continued complaining, Also, I can't believe neither of you knows that saying. It's: If a tree falls in the forest and nobody's around to see, does it make any sound? There's a different one about the pope and the woods. Something to do with a bear.

Thanks, Encyclopedia Brown. Mikey rolled his eyes. Nerds.

I tossed the phone over the back of the couch, and it bounced straight off onto the floor. Oops. The aggravated expression on D's face made Mikey crack up again. This time I joined him.

When the doorbell rang, I volunteered to go let Aaron in. Darius's mom, holding a tablet and trailed by their fluffy labradoodle-y dog, was halfway to the front door when I took a short run on the cold tiles and slid by in my socks. I grabbed the handles to the tall double doors and pulled. So bright outside, I had to squint.

Aaron tucked his skateboard under his arm and said, as he pulled off his hat and gloves, Your buddy MIKEY nearly got me shot! You all know Black boys can't be walking up to no strangers' houses.

But he was grinning as he shivered his way into the house, so I figured he wasn't too torn.

Did you actually walk into a stranger's house? I asked, and Aaron shook his head.

I can read, he said. No Delicious on the mailbox.

But you can't follow a GPS, I said.

Aaron grinned and hauled a heavy-looking backpack higher on his shoulder.

We passed the kitchen and Mrs. Delicious, who had settled there with her tablet, did a double take and said, Skateboards, bikes. I can't believe you boys going 'round in this cold! It's not June.

Mikey and Darius had gone ahead and chosen the first movie. Fine with me. After a round of hand-claps/finger-twists/fist-taps, D grabbed the remote that controlled the player and light and the heat and whatnot, and a pale square grew on the lowered movie screen.

Nobody'd mention it, but all of us hanging at D's showed how differently we lived. Darius's parents made a mint. His house had a big wooden play set nobody used anymore ('cept the zip line) and a pool curved like a jelly bean, outdoor sound system hidden in fake rocks. It was wild 'cause, near the train station, Mikey's apartment was crammed with his sibs and some gator-faced dogs. Aaron lived closer to me in a town house with his brother, neat-freak grandma, and sometimes dad. Stuff-wise, even with all the sibs and pets and parents, the three of us could fold up easy and fit in the wallet of Darius's life.

I passed Aaron a mini box of Lemonheads and Mikey exclaimed, It's like I SAID. If the pope FARTS in the woods, does anybody CARE?

Aaron screwed up his face and shifted his eyes to Darius, then to me like, I miss something? Silence. Mikey and D and me held it in till we couldn't. Then we roared and Darius pounded Mikey's back when he choked on a Mike and Ike or something.

Y'all is crazy, said Aaron.

* * *

First movie was all Mikey. Fast cars, dudes with arms made for popping people's heads off. Girls with hair sliding around as they tilted pointy side smiles toward the dudes. After the first car exploded into a fiery fireball, a rustling made me look up. Aaron unzipped his backpack. Inside, silver cans caught the light bouncing back from the projector screen.

I squinted. My mouth dropped open.

Aaron whispered to Mikey, Got ya somethin'.

I wasn't the only one who heard. Cars halted mid-leap. Vin Diesel paused.

What the heck? Darius said as Mikey pulled the bag wider, revealing six shiny beers.

We talked about this, D complained. What did I say?

With a glint in his eye I recognized from candy snatching, Aaron shrugged. He told us, You said MIKEY better not bring any beer. Good thing my name ain't Mikey.

Aaron and Mikey high-fived.

My MOM is upstairs? Darius gestured. And you do know we're twelve, right?

Aaron and Mikey glanced at each other, Aaron fixing his mouth so it seemed less smiling. D tried to pull me into an eye lock, but I avoided everyone.

How she gonna know, you don't tell her? Mikey said.

She'll smell it.

She a bloodhound? Aaron laughed. How she gonna sniff way upstairs and 'cross the house? This place is a cruise ship! And like a cruise, it ain't a party if we ain't got drinks. I brought good stuff— not that pee Mikey drinks.

Whatever, Mikey said. Beer is beer.

I said no. Darius stood up and tightly crossed his arms.

Aaron added, My brother made me pay twice what these cost, and then I had to haul 'em to your place on my skateboard, up here in the boonies! Cut me some slack, bruh.

Darius jabbed the remote and the projector started a countdown. He said, This movie marathon is canceled.

Awww! Aaron whined. C'mon, dude.

Stop being a punk, Mikey said as he stood up with eyes narrowed. Always worried about gettin' in trouble. Like anything'll happen. What's Momma gonna do, take away your two hundred video games?

When Aaron followed suit, standing, D glanced at me again.

I said, Sit down, people, c'mon.

Mikey wasn't having it. He grabbed the remote, jammed a bunch of buttons, and noise exploded from the hidden sound system. Men on screen started to shout at each other while Mikey stepped into Darius's face. Surprised, Aaron and me met eyes. *What's about to happen here?*

Hold on, hold on, Aaron said, half raising a hand like to grab Mikey.

Mikey pressed in closer. Anybody who wants a beer gets one. Just keep it out of sight. Now SIT, boo-boo.

Mikey prodded Darius's chest and D's jaw locked. I waited for the shoving to begin.

D, I said, keeping my butt glued to the cushion. It's not like . . . weed, or whatever.

What you know about some weed? Aaron half laughed.

Ignoring him, I reached to pry the remote from Mikey and pause the movie. Tossing the remote to Darius, who of course fumbled it, I ignored Mikey's glare. He wouldn't challenge me the same as with DD. I hit harder.

Kinda pissed me off, Mikey acting like he had all the power. If he said, Nah, put the beers away, Aaron would. Not a word more. How come Mikey was so good at getting people to follow him when he mostly led them off cliffs?

Silence. Four dudes stiller than shadow, faces sliced with light or dark, depending where we were in the room.

Finally, I asked, We here to watch movies? Or we here to fight?

We're not gonna get you busted, Double D, Aaron said. What you take us for? Amateurs?

He headed over and pulled out two beers, popped the tabs, handed one to Mikey, and looked at me. I shook my head once. Hardly liked the champagne Dad gave sips of on New Year's Eve.

Darius frowned. He turned a mutinous expression on Aaron before catching my eyes one last time.

Raising my chin, I silent-spoke: Your call, D. Kick us out? Brawl with Mikey, here and now? Rip us into twin orbits, shooting away from each other?

Darius pivoted from Mikey's flared nostrils and stomped to the farthest point of the couch. Nothing happened for a moment, then his arm swung up. Soft click from the remote.

*　*　*

Aaron's choice, big surprise, included a whole buncha boys talking tough, fighting disgusting alien things with pincher-legs, and racing around a maze with stone walls taller than some buildings in

New York. At one point, while Darius and me smacked on candy, and Aaron and Mikey took near-silent swigs, D's hairy dog pressed her cold, damp nose under my ear, shocking the bejesus out of me. I yelped and the boys shouted. Laughing washed away some of Darius's funk, Mikey's grump.

We took a breather between the second and third movie. I was glad. My gut had started to twist with the endless helplessness, the running away. Watching these kinds of movies didn't usually make me feel so weird. I didn't like it.

Man, I forgot how banging your sound system is! It's like being in a real theater. Aaron clapped Darius on the shoulder as everyone stood to stretch and grab more food.

I wandered to the back of the room, where Ms. Pac-Man now seemed more appealing: those cute blipping noises. No explosions. No curdling screams.

Mikey interrupted my thoughts. Want to go a round?

We sat at the low console and Darius offered up the red Solo cup of quarters his family keeps in the room so we can play without paying. The four of us got a solid team tournament going. Team A: Mikey and me totally whooping Team B: Darius and Aaron's butts. Darius's mom visited as we were winding down, and I saw both Darius and Aaron sneak glances at the couch, where he'd thrown an accent pillow over his backpack. We all breathed relief when

Mrs. Delicious left, the dog following with lazy-wagging tail, nails clicking on the glossy stairs.

Being in the basement meant no windows, and I missed seeing the sky do its slow fade. On the Saturdays I spent with C., when the day stretched long and the blinds sliced the porch with shade and sun, we'd yank hoodies over our heads, or wear Tío's old flannels, and hit the wilderness for some Wiffle-rock. I could almost hear C.'s voice calling as she tossed a lumpy stone: Miss, miss, swing batter batter! Almost feel the crisp stab of frozen air in my lungs.

Hey, said a voice near my ear. Earth-to-Jonas-son.

I blinked at Aaron waving his hand in front of my face.

He grinned. Candy coma?

I heard Mikey whine, Man, I can't believe you got us in here watching a movie about females.

Darius eyed him. *Kill Bill* is a gruesome opus of quasi-feminist vengeance that marginally subverts the misogynistic discourse of typical Hollywood fare. Also, it's funny and there's a lot of swords.

Mikey threw his head over the back of the couch. Oh. God. Booooring!

Of course, because Mikey complained, the final movie jammed my gut from the get-go. Not a thing went down could happen in real life, nohow, but I still felt weird. Started to sweat. Started to remember.

Who made spit leap from her mouth, fist to the jaw? (Not me—dude in the movie.)

Who gave chase? (Me. But it was a different girl. A kid my age. Looked like a hill of clothes, running away.)

Who got a sword from an old guy who seemed kinda magic? (C'mon. Nobody. Movie make-believe.)

Who had her down on the ground? (Was that me?)

Who sliced up a bunch of guys in suits? (For reals?)

Who heard her cry stop? Stop.

Stop.

When the girl ran, who went after because the ground made a hollow sound and shadows leaped like they do if it's a perfect Halloween, and who kicked her feet from under her so she tumbled but held her wrists so the asphalt rose slower? (Nobody knows. She wouldn't've. I was wearing a ski mask.)

Who went down, too? Who also said stop? (Stop!) Who said, I'm not playing?

Where did the mask go? (Gone. Gideon made it a shadow in the road.)

Who said, Stop hollering. Stop trying to hit me. I'll let you go?

Next I knew, my legs were standing. In the real world, my real feet walked me toward the door at the back of the room, past shiny black cabinets with bottles in more shapes and sizes than were in Aaron's backpack, into the tiny bathroom that I'd only seen once before, when it was an emergency (we weren't allowed to mess with the bar at the very back of the room, behind the foosball table).

That movie's nothing like real life. I washed my hands three times. When I returned, Mikey flashed his teeth: Scared? I flipped him the bird.

I had to do something to get through. I applied the strategy I'd taught Rex and played Guess the Background Instruments. When that stopped helping, I unfocused my eyes but stared straight ahead while sweat trickled down my ribs under my sweater.

Finally. Finally, Darius hit the lights button on the remote and Aaron and Mikey jumped straight in, talking over each other, describing what was stupid or impossible, or what should've happened. I tried to act normal as I waited for my heart to quit hammering and checked my phone for the time. It was an hour later than I said I'd leave.

We need to straighten this place before Mom sees. Darius gazed bleary-eyed at the scattered candy wrappers, crumbs across the couch, DVD cases on the floor. And Aaron, you need to pack up all your stupid beer crap first.

Pack the crap! Aaron said, and giggled.

Mikey grinned lopsidedly, watching Aaron but not helping. He swayed when he turned to look over what was left on the foosball table.

I gotta jet, I told them as I gathered all the snacks. Darius, I'll take these up to the kitchen and go from there?

Yeah, yeah. Darius waved at me. See you at school tomorrow.

Yo, we gotta do another movie marathon! Aaron declared, pounding Darius on the back. That was awwwwesome.

Everyone agreed, so I did, too. I was lying.

* * *

Looks like someone's hard at work. Mom appeared over my shoulder.

I hadn't heard her approach from the top of the stairs after Rex answered the door. *Not supposed to be here.* I kept my eyes glued to Dad's laptop, science book open nearby and a marked-up essay for English spread across the big leather ottoman / coffee table.

Mom said, How about a Hi, Mom?

Hi, I mumbled.

Mom waited a moment before making her favorite sound: Mmm!

While I pretended my homework was so riveting I couldn't tear myself away if bears ran through, Mom left me for people more interested. Rex switched her talk-bazookas on full blast, rendering me invisible. I looked out the window at the dark river. The scene in the reflection: Dad + Mom = half hug, no kiss = good. Rex: yak yak school yak yak in swim class I'm graduating to a clown fish yak yak.

It felt weird having Mom in the space, like we for no good reason transplanted our family to a place where we don't fit and are even more likely to fight. *Plus, there was Friday.*

Ugh. I shook my head to dislodge gross thoughts and popped up to help set the table before Dad called over. While Rex handled forks/spoons/knives, Mom perched on the edge of a kitchen stool. She crossed her legs at the ankles and smiled, head tilted so her gold hoop earrings (which baby Rex used to pull) swung, catching the light.

Plates clicked as "cool jazz" played from the radio in the kitchen after a long period of a dull DJ going on and on. Wine for the Adults, sparkling juice for the Kids. We blessed. Mom knocked back wine before anyone took a bite, and Rex restarted the yak yak yak till I wanted to dive for her mouth with packing tape.

Mom, I said, interrupting Rex's endless story about each and every kid who got in trouble in her class (except her, so told).

Hey, Bear. Mom eye-smiled at me, though she'd acted annoyed five minutes before when I didn't greet her exactly how she wanted. Probably the wine.

Uh-oh, said Dad. Here it comes.

Mom paused in the middle of spearing green beans on her fork. Uh-oh, what?

Jonas is about to ask you to lay bare the secrets of your childhood, Dad said.

I glared at him.

Go ahead, Dad prodded. Ask.

Never mind, I muttered.

No you don't, Dad said. Fair's fair! Ask your mother what you asked me.

You never answered! I said.

You wouldn't let me, Dad countered. I'm not gonna be the only one subjected to this!

I heaved a huge sigh, all attention on me. Rex shook her head, but nothing I could do now. My plan hadn't been to ask *that*, especially after last time.

What's like . . . the worst thing you ever did? I said.

Dad laughed like I'd said something funny. Mom cut her eyes at him.

C'mon, Olivia. Dad grinned. Be a good sport. Answer your son.

Why are you so delighted by this? Mom said. What's your answer, Tru?

I butted in, When you were my age, I meant.

When I was twelve? Mom hesitated and sipped her wine. She said, I'll tell you. I know you'd never, ever behave that way. I threw my sister through a window.

Rex's mouth dropped open.

Through a window? I repeated. Like a glass window?

You're joking! Dad said. Adelaide or Demi?

Your aunt Demi, Mom told us. It was summer, so there was just a screen. Demi went straight through. Good thing we were on the first floor—she landed on the porch.

Did she get hurt bad? Rex asked.

Mom laughed. No. It was more of a shock than anything else. Water under the bridge now. Your grandma was still alive then. She made me pay for the screen, which took *weeks* of babysitting. Aunt Demi got me back . . . eventually. That's a tale for another day. Tru, you're up.

Oh, no. Dad spread his hands. I plead the Fifth.

Don't even, Mom groaned.

The fifth what? Rex asked.

I do and I will, Dad said over her head to Mom.

Truman, I *shared*. Mom made go-on movements with her hands.

Nooooope.

Oh, come on. You're the one always saying we need to expose the kids to reality!

I never said we needed to tell them everything. Dad lifted his wine and took a slow, satisfied sip.

Mmm. Mom folded her lips in and narrowed her eyes the way my sister does (which reminds you she's not called Rex for nothing).

Here we go, I thought.

Don't be like that, Olivia, Dad said, setting his glass down. We're having fun. Don't turn it into something else.

Having fun? Mom rolled her eyes so hard, practically heard them click. Uh, no, Tru. I believe what you're doing is called *withholding*.

Why's this about me all of a sudden? I didn't ask the question.

Rex and me exchanged glances. Without my asking, kid sister slid me her plate.

Our parents were now leaning toward each other over the table, both armed with wine.

Dad said, I don't understand why you keep on with this, O. You repeat this pattern—

Standing, I said excuse me to no one who'd listen and bumped Rex with my elbow. We fled to the kitchen, where I turned on the faucet full blast to drown out the growing argument.

When we were littler, before they split, Rex'd come crawling into my bed and I'd crank the forest-sounds function on my clock radio when the muffled buzz of our parents' arguing grew into shouting. I'd feel Rex's heart beating hard as she pressed against me while I read aloud whatever book or crap I dug from the piles on my floor.

Could've been worse. They never hit each other or threw stuff like in other kids' houses. Shouting eventually become cold, heavy silence.

Tonight, our parents would probably snap at each other till somebody called truce. Then Mom would leave and Dad would apologize, like usual. They're as bad as kids. At the sink, I rubbed a limp, mildew-smelling sponge in circles, then handed the dripping plate to Rex for drying.

Seeing how her face was set, I wished I could tell my sister, You like to have them together but this is exactly why Mom should NOT come here.

Little things become big things, just like that.

Chapter 10
BAILING

Gideon with an ax. Gideon at my locker with an ax. I've got nothin'. My heart clutches. It's slipping, heavy.

I've got a plastic bat. Yellow. Smells hollow as I twist my fists on the handle. I wave it high.

Gideon at my locker with socks static-clinging to her shirt. Also a bra. I try not to stare at the bra. I feel too warm, and embarrassed. Next somehow, she's peering out through the locker slits. Dark eyes. Red metal.

Someone starts screaming. Is it her?

Mist rolls and Rex and Dad and me see the deer. When my sister points, we leap, forelegs pressed to our chests.

I say, Fire-breathing deer: ridiculous.

Dad says, We're not going to make it.

My eyes popped open like somebody pressed a button on my head. Scrubbing my hands through my hair and over my face, I sat up and looked across my bedroom at the clock. Two tiny shadows swirled in the fish tank beside it. I had a good four hours left before school.

I lay back down. Sat up again and patted the dark floor beside my bed until I touched a sweatshirt. Pulling it over my head, I felt better, warmer. I climbed out of bed to sit in my hard plastic desk chair. When I switched on the lamp, Swimmy and Alex came to see what was up. I watched them, attempting to read their fishy minds until my eyes felt gritty.

Back in bed, tossing, I pictured Mikey and the boys. Gideon and the notes. My parents, Stew and Anthony, Robin and Rex. How many people would I disappoint if they learned what happened with me and Gideon on Halloween? Every day was one day further away, one less reason to care. So why was I starting to care?

I finally admitted that sleep had left the room and wasn't coming back. Out of bed again, I dredged the floor for something to read. Nada. Next, picking through the pile of papers on my desk, I pulled out a zine from Robin's collection that I still hadn't delivered to C. This one, surprisingly, didn't have bad art or swears. Flipping through, I spun my chair seat in a creaking circle. A coupla ideas caught me, stopped me short. I stopped spinning, straightened out of my slump, and turned the little booklet to look at the cover, which showed a drawing of teens with their arms around each other, grinning peachily under a handwritten title:

A Young Person's Guide to Consent for Every Body

Mom kept books about bodies and puberty or whatever on a shelf in the den where Rex and me could get 'em anytime we wanted, but this zine felt different.

Maybe, I told myself, there's something here that'll tell if I'm a kid who just got carried away, or if I'm worse.

I abandoned the desk and quietly shut my bedroom door. Sitting cross-legged on the carpet and scooting till my back pressed against the wood, I opened the zine again and leaned low in the lamp-spotted dark to read.

* * *

The PROBLEM, Charity barked, is that you and your BOYS been looking too HARD. PEOPLE are starting to NOTICE.

When I dragged myself into school on Monday morning, I hadn't known I needed a plan. Apparently, I did because here was O'Dell in my ear, and here I was without a way to hold her off, whatever she was on about.

Sighing, I spun the three-part combo. The best I could manage was: What?

I glanced at her. My eyes traveled from the twinkle of her pink nails with tiny embedded gems, up the thick wrist, to the arm in a pink sleeve, to the face with its flaring nostrils and pink lip gloss. Charity O'Dell, practically on top of me.

Charity said: Tell me what you and your nappy-headed friends were doing up in Gideon Rao's yard?

I said: . . . ? (Who's nappy?)

I said: Didn't happen.

Charity said: Somebody told me that somebody ELSE saw you and your little buddies in her neighborhood, and I KNOW that's where you went because the bunch of you all been whispering about that girl all week.

I allowed my eyes to flick in her direction. I squinted. I said, Today is Monday.

Charity: You know what I mean. Last week.

Me: Wait. Somebody saw us at Gideon's house last week?

Me (tired brain: *click, click, click*):

Me: Oh. Yeah, that was Mikey and Darius, but they were in the bushes.

Charity: It doesn't matter where they were! They were THERE.

Me (removing books from my locker): Doesn't matter? Oh. Okay. So why are we talking about this?

I considered the books already in my backpack and was reaching to do something with something when she leaned in threateningly, lips twisting as she *smack-smack*ed some gum.

I said, Gum's banned in school.

Then I opened my locker door wider to block her face.

Bam! Charity's girly hand battered the metal door.

She said, You'd better TALK to me, JONAS. Is Mikey macking on that girl or WHAT?

My heart jumped a little (Mikey and Gideon?) and I said, What?

Charity added, low, She's nothing special, so I don't know why y'all are suddenly all about her. Skinny thing. Like a TWIG.

I huffed, half grinning. You are barking up the wrong tree, girl. That's not why they were there.

Charity leaned in so close I smelled the fakest fruit scent ever existed, and hissed, Why. Were. They. There?

Charity and Mikey were two bad peas in a rotten pod; nothing I said could spoil them more. Let 'em fall off the vine.

Shaking my head and shutting my locker, I asked, Who saw them?

The bell rang, startling us both, and I stepped backward into the laser light of two glaring eyeballs—Mikey. Great.

Hall monitors' voices started calling out threats as I inched away, toward homeroom. In just a few moments, VP Hong would appear like a clockwork bird shooting out on the hour. Charity was backing off as well, her expression wary.

I said the only thing left worth saying: Ask him yourself.

*　*　*

Ask him yourself. Riiiiight.

Charity O'Dell and Mikey were squaring off in the lunchroom. Mikey's perfect plaits looked shiny in the terrible fluorescent light; his chin was ducked low as Charity barked, her hand flying out and accusing this, that, and the other thing. I couldn't completely make out what they were saying, and I hoped I wouldn't need to.

Add to that, Gideon in my side view. Why? Girl and I mostly ignored each other since Halloween, except for the deal with the ball at recess. Now I couldn't stop seeing her. Seemed she was TRYING to trip me up, to spook me.

Each time I turned away or swiveled around or bit my pen and

pretended to be thinking, gazing off so it didn't seem like I was staring. My pen tasted gross, but in less than five hours, I'd discovered
a bunch of things, such as:

- Gideon Rao's ears are small, pointy-tipped, and kind of
  stick out. She wears a single dangly-sparkly earring in her
  right ear but nothing in the left. (Fell out?)

- At recess, girl can play a mean game of four square if she
  wants, against anybody who steps, boy or girl.

- Unlike Charity's crew, Gideon and pals travel between
  classes without hollering, hooting, or swishing their butts.

- In science, she's still paying more attention to the paperback hidden in her lap. Though today had the correct
  answer when Mrs. White came calling.

- When Gideon wraps her black braids into two glossy buns,
  a fringe of loose hair hangs down the back of her neck.

- Monday's outfit includes dark brown tights, boots, and a
  retro blue sweatshirt with a howling wolf in front of a
  moon.

Wolf? I said to myself. C'mon. More like a deer, tail flipped white,
bounding away. I'M the wolf.

That thought gave me a funny pang, so I put it away and glanced at Double D on the other side of the table, though I had to adjust my sight so I stopped seeing Gideon beyond with that one group of kids I can never tell what race they are.

Darius noticed where my eyes were being pulled and said, Your specimen is curious.

I groaned. Can you not say things like that?

He shrugged over the black quinoa salad his mom packed AGAIN and he couldn't trade because not a single kid would eat that nonsense.

D: You're turning into a real scientist. Observing all the time.

Me: How would you know since you're busy Minding Your Own Business? Hint-HINT. And what is that you're eating? Birdseed?

D: Quinoa is the superfood of the Andes. Mom's obsessed. C'mon, Jonas. Describe the binomial nomenclature of your specimen.

Me: What? The bio-what?

Mikey (erupting from nowhere to smack his hand down on the table):

D (gasping, coughing as birdseed gets stuck in his throat):

Me: Mikey, what the—?

Mikey (hissing): Why'd you tell HER about . . . G's place? You stupid?

Me (standing, because can't let a dude tower): What? Which her?

Mikey: You know which HER. Now she's pissed.

Me (good):

Me: What was I supposed to say? Charity asked me. Plus, sounded like she already knew.

Mikey: You didn't have to confirm it.

Me: Well, how's your getting loud gonna make Charity any less mad? She's right over there. Girl's got ears like a bat.

I glanced quickly around the lunchroom. In the far corner, the hunkered deer. A few tables over, Charity sure enough watching us with crafty, glittering eyes while the girls around her fluttered and changed positions like little birds gathering in the bushes. Everybody somebody's friend. At each door, a teacher or a monitor, standing tall in dark pants, blazers, and long lanyards with their IDs attached, drinking tall coffees.

Not wanting to get caught, I dropped back down on the glossy, hard chair. Mikey was up now and not about to go down as easy as me—let 'em get caught. Instead of engaging in an evil-eye lock, I turned to my sandwich, a little lumpy now because I'd accidentally squeezed it. I was considering which lump to bite when, without warning, Mikey leaned forward and flat-palm whacked the side of my head. Not crazy-hard, but startling. I teleported out of my seat into Mikey's face. Within a second, Dr. Adeyemo was in mine.

Hey, hey, hey! he barked as he pulled me back. I saw that. Mikey Hill, you know that striking someone is against school conduct. Pack your things and come with me. Jonas Abraham, you—

Dr. Adeyemo, I interrupted. I didn't do anything! I was just sitting here.

Mikey snarled, Don't fake, JONAS!

STOP. Dr. Adeyemo put a hand up. Hill, go with the monitor. I'll speak with you shortly. Be glad it's me who saw this and not VP Hong.

After Mikey stomped away, teacher dropped his sights to me and Double D; might not have been breathing, he was so still.

Not my fault, I said, rubbing the side of my head. He did that unprovoked!

Dr. Adeyemo frowned. What kind of example are you setting, Mr. Abraham? Mr. Delicious?

Darius ducked his head even lower. I followed his example. Maybe if I seemed embarrassed, Dr. Adeyemo wouldn't make me sit in the office across from a PO'd Mikey. Stewing until VP called each of us in to hear the story of how we ended up in her office . . . again.

Sorry, Dr. A., I said.

Teacher knelt to stare me and DD in the eyes for a long moment.

He said, This type of behavior doesn't only reflect on you. Every other student of color, the whole school community—they're watching, learning. You're upper-school students! Use the gifts that you have here—he tapped my temple lightly with two fingers—and here—he tapped my chest. Do better.

Dr. Adeyemo rose and said in a louder voice, I'm splitting you up. Mr. Delicious, remain here. Mr. Abraham, move to that table. And Mr. Abraham, you and Mr. Hill should think about bringing your issue to a circle before things go too far. Think about it.

I sat alone until the bell rang. Dr. A.'s suggestion reminded me of community service with Mrs. White, when I considered asking her for help. The moment passed then, like now, leaving behind the question: What's the point? Mikey's a pain, but dudes be like that. What would sitting around in a circle complaining about it fix?

I stood to fall in / head out and someone brushed close. Figured it was Charity but nope: Gideon and her buddies. As they passed, Gideon threw me a glare that, if it was a fireball, would have roasted me and gone on to fry a few other kids. Bell rang and I escaped to class feeling tired, burnt, and a few other things.

* * *

I jammed a cold empanada in my mouth and spoke around it. Big bowla cat food your latest project? How you plannin' to save the world w'at?

C., who was trying to stuff her hair in her hoodie without touching it with paste-covered fingers, tossed me a look.

Nearby, on the kitchen counter, girl's homework seemed to involve a super-size mixing bowl and a cat as Cuidado stuck his pink nose in and started to lap. The smell was thick and sweet in a stuffy, newspaper-y way. Nothing I'd eat but: cats = weird = that's just how it is.

Outside their little house, the sun sank down, down, down and I knew Mom wasn't gonna love me not being home already, but Tío Rodrigo was usually happy enough to drive me home. Hard for Mom to stay annoyed if I was out doin' something that helped keep my grades up.

Noooo, Jonasito, C. said. OBVIOUSLY. Y'know, you could put tu imaginación to better use. Like, that zine page, for example. What you sent me—it's okay, better'n the stuff about your sister . . . but it's not a hundred percent. Le falta algo.

I stopped chewing and glanced through the doorway to the cramped dining room where Tío sat typing, paper and books stacked around him. Hopefully concentrating too hard to overhear. And anyway C. had music going on her phone, some mopey folk stuff.

What Roxita wrote, though . . . , C. said, her face lighting with a smile.

I grinned back. I know, right? SHE BROKE EVERY GLASS.

We looked at each other and laughed. C. spun to bump the cat with her elbow.

Cuidado! C. growled, then asked, Did she really?

I shrugged and bit into a second empanada—fried, cheesy goodness. I made my way to the table, on the way scooping the cat and dropping him to the floor.

I wasn't there, I said. But we never use any fancy glasses, so . . .

Inspecting seven paper-covered balloons sitting lumpily beside the sink, I couldn't begin to figure out what girl was up to. Before I asked, C. flipped the switch on her mood.

Stop trying to distract me by talking about Roxita's page, she said. What about yours? When're you gonna do it up?

What do you mean? I asked as I considered my math homework. I made it on the zine machine. Just like Stew and Robin said. Don't see how it could be better. Bad enough you got me tellin' about stuff nobody needs to hear.

No one *will*, C. reminded me. It's gonna be—

Anónimo, I finished for her. Yeah, yeah. I know. Can we listen to something else? I'm tired of your Theo Christmas guy.

Still kinda nervous, I spied Tío Rodrigo not-listening to us. Time to crank the noise and block him for sure. *A kid can't be too careful.* The tinny Bluetooth speaker was spotted with dots of paste.

C. nodded. I popped up, asking, Where's your phone?

She bumped out her skinny hip and said, Pocket.

As I reached to grab the phone, a weirdness wound 'round my gut like a cat weaving through my legs. It squeezed. I stopped.

Put on Shakira, C. said as she swayed and made a target out of her pocket.

Shaking my head, I moved to pluck the phone away and paused again. Normally, I'd never touch C. there. I'd say: Get it yourself.

That zine from Robin's pile . . . C. and I obviously weren't about boy-girl stuff. Still. What if she felt funny about me reaching in her pocket?

Hey! C. peered over her shoulder. Earth to Jonasito!

Huh? I said like I hadn't frozen with my hand out.

Screw it, I thought. Weirder to hover than do what she asked.

C.'s pocket was snug and once I grabbed the phone, she bounced back to her bowl of goop, unfazed. I scrolled. Spanish yodeling burst from the speaker. Rubbing my hand across my hip, I launched into the first thing on my mind, which happened to be the last thing I wanted to discuss.

You know I'm not an artist, I said.

Who said you need to be? C. said as she dipped a long strip of paper into the paste bowl and laid it across a balloon. You read what I loaned you?

I nodded. She didn't need to know I'd flipped through only the one. Also, that zine from Robin, which was the whole reason I'd felt weird about digging in C.'s pocket. A person can't unread stuff. Probably true of what I wrote, too. Too late to back out?

I said, Explain how this is gonna do anybody any good. Can't we write about something else? Like, I don't know, unicorns?

No, C. said. Okay, picture this: a snow pile. Pretend the snow is stories. A whole bunch of snows—stories—together until es más grande. The hill gets packed, and people climb and their feet stop sinking 'cause it's, how do you say? ¿Presionada? Pressed . . . ?

Packed down? I offered.

¡Sí, sí! C. said, making shapes with her dripping hands. Picture this: layers, each, eh, snowflake is different. Each layer is different.

That's how the zine is. Small stuff, big stuff . . . juntos. Together.

And what? I said. People sled down? That doesn't even make sense.

Unicorns is kid stuff, C. said. That's *ppfffffftttt*, flat like a pancake. When Tío writes, my mamita writes, there's *fltfltflt* layers with air between. The zine has layers; your story is a layer, sí poh?

I guess, I said.

Sliding my math aside, I knelt on a chair (which Mom never let me do at home). Drumming my knuckles against the table, I listened to Tío slam-typing in the dining room like he'd mistaken his laptop for a zine machine. Nearby C. pasted to the beat of Shakira! Shakira!

I stared at my knuckles, my hands. *I had fists.* Why'd I do it, back in October, on Halloween? *She was running. I was running.*

Pulling a notebook toward me, I scribbled: People get carried away. Then I was off, writing.

C: You just including
one, right?

—JA

I DON'T KNOW WHY I DID IT

I don't know why I did it. She was running. I was running.
People get carried away. That's what Mom says: You're getting
carried away.

There was a bright moon, perfect for Halloween. Everybody
could see anything.

I grabbed the girl. We fell.

Fell like a movie where a lady gets killed at the beginning.
She's screaming and screaming. Earlier, running and tripping
because of high heels. Drops her purse and stuff falls out,
rolling away like candy. You can't feel bad because why didn't
she wear sneakers?

On the ground, the girl didn't scream. She had no voice. She
had elbows and fists. I had no voice. I had my heart jumping
out my throat. Her fingers dragged my ski mask, hot cloth
jerked my chin.

I had fists. Couldn't/shouldn't use them.

Slamming. It was an accident. Night went still.

Who cares about Movie Lady? People wanna see the rest:
who dies, who lives. A good movie is more than one person
screaming.

Candy stomped and shattered,
not really candy anymore.

Chapter 11
LAYERS

Stew walked past in his bright orange sneakers and flipped the sign on the door from OPEN to CLOSED, PLEASE CALL AGAIN.

What does that even mean? I asked as I set the label maker down. Call again?

Tuesdays were slow at Soho, not that I was usually working. Still finding reasons to avoid spending too much time with Dad, I'd convinced Stew to let me hang if I finished up my homework first.

Now I stood at the front, greeting the nonexistent customers. Also, I was printing out labels and trying different combos on a sheet of scrap paper. Can't draw worth a lick, but there's a whole stockroom here full of random things nobody wants to buy—flashy silver paper, stickers, fancy hole punches, paper clips shaped like snails. Some weird combo could make C. happy. Problem was, what I'd written wasn't like . . . jolly. Candy snatching was fun, but also serious.

I sighed. Why was I bothering with this?

Stew passed me again, going the other way.

He said, It's a phrase from a long time ago. Like, hitch yer horse to that rail yonder, strut outta a saloon with your spurs janglin'. Call again!

Mmm, I said, and typed into the label maker: **yonder**. I hit print.

You 'bout ready to go, little man? It's six, Stew said, disappearing into the back room.

Mmm-hmm, I replied, and typed: **WHOOP!** I hit print.

As the machine sputtered out a thin white strip, I checked that my backpack was behind the counter with me. Yup. I typed: **thump-thumpTHUMP**. I hit print.

Stew returned, stepped behind the counter with me, and slid a floppy, bow-shaped cloth barrette into his hair to put up his bangs so they couldn't annoy him while he was doing the register. Purple and sparking, it definitely belonged to Rex. She'd freak if she saw Stew wearing it casual-like (I'd never tell her).

I typed: **FREAK OUT**. I typed: **screaming**. I typed: **candy**. I typed: **stars**. Print print print.

Your dad coming to get you? Stew asked. Or am I driving you home?

I pulled out my phone and checked the messages.

Mom: Change of plans, baby bear. You're here tonight b/c Dad's in a crunch w/ work before the holiday. Dropped Rex off earlier. Where are you?

Mom: Bear. It's getting late. Hope you're not out skateboarding on a SCHOOL NIGHT.

Mom: Jonas, you are where?

Dad: Check in w/Mom, ok?

I put thumbs to phone and shot off messages to both.

You're driving me home, I informed Stew before turning back to the label maker.

I typed: **the worst thing I ever did**. Print.

Stew's counting aloud filled the store. I glanced out the window at the dark street. Someone was approaching the shop, walking fast. If they'd checked the website, or tried to call, they'd know we close at six p.m. on Tuesdays. Too bad for them.

I typed: **was also the most fun**. Print.

You're gonna pay for those? Stew asked, shooting me a side-eye. Think we're made of label tape?

I shrugged. I said, there were rolls and rolls more in the back.

Yeah? Stewart smiled. You think it grows on trees? Huh? Just, blowing around and free?

I wasn't gonna respond, but he stuck out his tongue and crossed his eyes, raspberrying like how he used to when Rex and me were little, and I couldn't hold back my laugh.

BAMBAM! We both jumped. I looked out. The face at the door was Mikey's.

What the heck? I said.

Isn't that your friend? Stew nudged me with his elbow.

I'ma head out for a bit, I said as I picked up my backpack, my coat stuffed inside.

Ten minutes, Stewart said. I'm almost done here.

I barely heard him as I made my way to the door and flipped the latch. Cold wrapped its fingers around and tried to poke through the cozy warmth inside Soho. I could see Mikey only had his thin jacket on, no hat and no gloves.

Hey, I said as I hefted the door wider. What's up? You wanna come in?

Yeah. Mikey's breath puffed, but soon as he stepped one foot in, he paused.

I followed his gaze to Stew and his bright hair and that dumb purple barrette.

Don't even start, I thought.

Mikey lifted his chin.

No, he said. Let's talk out here.

The urge to be killer stubborn welled up in me, so I asked, WHY?

Because. Mikey raised his voice, too. I don't wanna be TRAPPED in here with that FAG—

I shoved Mikey, and because he wasn't expecting it, he stumbled back a few steps.

Heeey! called Stew from inside.

I kept moving. It was hard not to push Mikey again, to not punch him in the face.

What's the matter with you? I demanded as I stalked away.

What is wrong with *you*? Mikey snapped back. I'm not the one always hanging 'round f—

STOP SAYING THAT! I shouted. Don't come over here saying that crap. Stew is *normal*. Stew is fine.

Mikey sucked his teeth. He is NOT fine. My brother says—

I don't care about your stupid brother!

Don't care about much, do you? Mikey said. You know what happened today, 'cause of you? School called my sister.

Okay. Your point?

Mikey huffed. People hurried past and not a single one pretended they weren't staring. Two boys like us, shouting in public on a Tuesday night? Yeah. People look.

You need to tell Adeyemo it was your fault, Mikey said.

I said, Dude. YOU hit ME.

Mikey: I popped you . . . but you started it. You need to tell that to Dr. A. so he lets me off the hook.

I shook my head. You're not making sense.

Mikey said, Look. You just need to talk to Adeyemo tomorrow, say it was a mistake so he can back off, and then my sister can lay off and not call my mom while she's . . . away. Okay?!

Away. Mikey's mother wasn't *away* on some vacation or business trip. She's been in prison since Mikey was a baby. Like C.'s mom, I've never met her. Mikey's sister is the one bossing them, leaning on Mikey's brother, Mikey, and his little sister to act right.

I crossed my arms. It's too late. I mean, you already hit me, and you said they called your sister. I bet your mom knows by now.

Mikey balled his hands. Come ON, Jonas! I ask you for ONE thing. You can't do this ONE thing? Ain't we friends?

He wasn't thinking straight. What could I say to convince the school? Me, who's already been in it a couple of times this year, who knocked Gideon off a wall, goofin', and then "forgot" to apologize because I guess I'm that kinda punk.

I stepped to the side to let a guy with a baby bundled in an umbrella stroller walk between us. Mikey barely moved. The stroller nicked his beat-up Nikes and guy muttered sorry, but Mikey was looking at his hands, which were shaking. Cold . . . or mad?

Boy said something hard to hear, so I leaned forward, stomping my feet to keep the blood moving.

I asked, What?

Mikey said, I helped you, man. Can't you return the favor?
I said, What? When?

Mikey looked up. Me and Darius, we ain't said nothing about Halloween. Aaron neither. You ain't even thankful.

I said, It's not the same thing! This is TO-TAL-LY different. Why should I lie if there's nothing I can do? For real? You think they'll listen to ME?

Mikey:

Mikey: Know what your problem is? You're soft.

Eyes narrowed, he jerked his chin at Soho. Maybe your babysitter'll help out next time you cross somebody. You can have a slap fight.

I told myself, He's trying to piss you off.

Dad-in-My-Head advised, Go for higher ground, Jonas.

I counted to myself, One . . . Two . . . Three . . .

Earlier I felt sorta bad that I hadn't sat down / shut up in the cafeteria. Now I needed to ghost before my body started making decisions for me, beginning with my fists.

I spun on my heels, swinging my backpack over my shoulder.

I didn't say, Sorry.

I didn't say, See you around.

Mikey shouted, Who's had your back since kiddiegarten? Who? Not that Bruce Lee fairy!

I flipped him the bird. Left without looking back. Surprised he didn't come at me.

* * *

We hadn't moved far from the shop. Three steps to the door and I pulled; of course the stupid thing was locked.

The sound of Mikey's bike wheeling away reached me across the wide sidewalk. I plucked my phone from my pocket. Dead. Won-der-ful.

What the heck, Stew? I said, wiggling my arm under the backpack strap.

I think they close at six, a woman behind me offered. You should try again tomorrow.

I wanted to say, I work here.

Said instead, Huh.

Reapplied myself loudly to the door. Probably Stew was in the stockroom with the music cranked. As I banged on the glass, palm flat, I saw from the side of my eye the woman and her gray-haired boyfriend hovering nearby. Waiting for my hoodlum self to break into a *paper* shop?

I felt tired. Why did everything have to be so hard?

When I heard the woman start to call out, Excuse me—? I spun on my heel, showing her my back.

Clapping to warm my hands on this weirdly freezing November night, I squinted down the street to see if light was shining out of North River Books. It was, yellow reflected warmly on the bricks beneath the tall windows.

I took a breath. One good thing.

North River Books was bustling for a Tuesday night. The front had people draped over every stuffed chair and more browsing the new, low-priced softcovers that sucker my mom into buying more than she intends. At the back, a crowd of people gathered like something interesting was about to happen.

I was bumped from behind. When I stepped out of the way, a hand grabbed my arm. I twisted fast and looked up into Robin McCormick's freckled face.

Jonas, she said, balancing the legs of two folding chairs on the toe of her boot. You here for the show?

I shook my head. C'I use the phone?

Sure. She nodded toward checkout, then hauled the folding chairs up off her toe.

Mind-Mama smacked me across the back of the head, and without wanting to, I found myself reaching to take the chairs.

Thanks. Robin sounded relieved. This event is bringing out the crowd, and we barely have enough staff scheduled. I need to help at the register. Drop these off at the back?

I delivered three rounds of two chairs each to where the cookbook and the travel shelves had been rolled away to make space. Setting them up in rows, I spied an event flyer in a plastic holder: Chelsea Rao, local producer, author, and music historian, debuting his book *Tabla on the Mountain: Weaving Together Traditions of Hindustani Classical and Modern American Rock*.

I thought, Chelsea? That's a girl's name. And Rao? Like Gideon Rao?

I needed to get out of there, stat. I basically teleported to checkout. A black cordless sat in a holder on the wall behind the counter. I pulled it out and realized that I didn't have Stew's number memorized.

Hey, Robin, I said, speaking around the other clerk, who had her hands full with a family of indecisive kids and their grumpy grandpa.

Robin was talking to a guy in a long, fancy white jacket with curlicues all over it, glasses, and faded jeans, saying, How's it looking, Chelsea?

The guy started telling Robin something, but all I heard was a loud buzzing in my ears 'cause there was an *actual* girl: skinny, shorter version of her dad with arms full of books, Chelsea's grinning face on the back cover. Gideon looked up and met my eyes straight on. ZING.

The world was a Rube Goldberg machine set into motion. I dropped low behind the counter, making Frowning Clerk jump and say, What the hell? Grumpy Grandpa responded, Excuse ME? The grandkids started shouting.

Curling down in the dust, near Frowning Clerk's boots, I asked myself, Why, why, WHY?

Above me, on the other side of the counter: Chelsea Rao, who played instruments no kid in my class could identify till Gideon showed up, and his kid (Gideon), both silent like maybe they weren't sure what was going on. Wasn't their eyes but Robin's that peered over and down.

Jonas, she said. What—?

The cordless phone was still pressed to my ear. Crazy as I must've looked, I hung on tight and made a slashing motion across my neck. Robin's eyebrows shot up. Her head disappeared. Over the pounding of my heart, I heard her say something to the Raos about where to set the books.

Huddled, I sucked in a loud breath. Guess I lived here now, among the forgotten paper clips and book dust. Frowning Clerk had a different opinion.

She said, GET. OUT. NOW.

＊　＊　＊

I bumped past Frowning Clerk, skirted Grumpy Grandpa and the Squealers, and made for the exit. Dodged the softcover tables and the rack near the door that held free catalogs and flyers, bookmarks, stuff. Before I touched the door handle, an arm swung up. I tweaked my trajectory, and somehow Robin snagged me anyway.

Zombies? Robin asked, spinning half-around as she dragged me to a halt. Poltergeists? You possessed, running through my store like your legs don't know how to walk? Why are you stealing the phone?

I glanced down. It was true. I handed her the cordless.

A second glance to the back of North River Books showed them all: Gideon, wearing a shining dress thing with pants and a gem in the middle of her forehead, talking to her dad; a high school boy with hair loose to his shoulders, who was thin like Gideon but much taller; and Mr. Rao, kneeling to unwrap a set of squat drums that looked like oversized acorns. Nearby, a woman who looked like an older, plump version of Gideon unpacked other instruments.

Stop pulling. Robin's voice brought me back and my eyes flicked to hers: hazel, narrowed, worried.

If I let your arm go now, she warned, you'll fall.

Instead, I yanked harder and slipped her grip. I spun, my face nearly hitting the glass door before I got my palms up to sound a loud *SMACK* against the glass, and tumbled outside.

Out on the sidewalk, my heart said *BAMBAMBAM*, but the sound wasn't nearly as loud as my name called across the bricks.

JONAS!

I turned and girl was there in her shining outfit and no coat, a few running steps past the yellow light thrown by North River Books. Eyes dark. Breathing in gulps—loud, harsh breaths. Or maybe that was me.

Gideon closed the distance to where I'd frozen on the sidewalk bump-out under the fancy streetlamp—one cold, black metal bench and giant terra-cotta pot. I didn't look at her. What could I say? I tucked my fists into my pits and swallowed.

Why are you here? she asked.

I shrugged, not knowing how to respond.

Why do you keep following me? She folded her arms, too.

I opened my mouth, but instead of asking, You crazy? in a voice that belonged to a weón who couldn't be bothered, who wasn't afraid of some girl, I blurted, Sorry!

Gideon took a step back.

Now it was Gideon asking, For what?

Then I seemed to be explaining how I wasn't the kind of guy who did stuff that ended in having to run from the law.

Listen, I said. At recess, that was lame. I'm really sorry about hitting you. But, uh, Mikey started it. Halloween, too. I mean candy snatching. I wouldn't want anybody treating my sister that way.

Her eyebrows wrinkled. She said, half laughing, What?

SORRY, I emphasized, taking a step forward. When we fought? I didn't mean that to happen.

For good measure, I added, And it was Mikey and Darius who toilet-papered your parents' car last week.

Gideon, called the boy who'd stood beside her in North River Books. Why are you out here?

Eyes boring into me, he continued in a rumbling voice too wide for his body. You know this guy?

Gideon looked at her brother. At me. Her lips pressed flat.

Here it is, I thought. Here we go.

A car horn blared and the three of us jumped about a mile. There was Stew, staring at me through the window of his Saab, holding his phone up to his ear. We watched him throw open the car door with a terrible metal screech that made us all lean back.

Stew half stood and shouted, There you are! Where have you *been*?

When I turned back to Gideon, her brother had thrown his jacket around her shoulders and was tugging her toward the store. Neither wasted a backward glance.

I let out a breath. ALL my breaths, actually.

Sweeping back his bangs, Stewart stalked around to the passenger side of his car and pulled open the door.

Get in, he said. Man, are you in trouble.

* * *

Rex was in the Best Mood Ever!!!!

After a tense car ride with Stew where he tore into me for wandering off, which had forced him to admit to my parents that he'd lost me, I was squeezed between his angry silence and Mom's PO'd texts that, luckily, I couldn't read yet 'cause my phone was still dead.

My sister, in the meantime, was in hog heaven. First, the parents had gone Full Fuss and it wasn't about her. Second, Rex loves a good last-minute switch in plans—gets the energy up, y'know. Third? Stew.

When he marched me through the mudroom into the kitchen, she started chanting his name. Then, while Mom scolded, kid wrapped both arms around Stew's beanpole self and beamed up at him.

Mom said, Why am I even paying for that phone if you don't have the decency to use it when it was most important?

She went on, And of course your father's work is more urgent than mine. My to-do list is JUST as long, but who do you see here making dinner, waiting to hear my son's excuse for being off the map. ON. A. SCHOOL. NIGHT.

Mom lifted her spatula and looked around at all of us like she wasn't sure who to swat first.

I raised my hands in surrender and, knowing good and well she wouldn't, said, You're not going to hit me with that?

Please, child, she said, and tossed the spatula on the counter. Stop trying to bait Stewart. He's not going to call Child Services.

Wiping pizza-y hands on her apron, Mom checked the oven. Basil and mozzarella smells wafted out before she let it slam shut.

Thank you, Stewart, Mom went on. For driving this ungrateful home. Do you need money for gas?

No thanks. Stew shook his head before shifting dark eyes in my direction. Jonas, you understand why we're upset, right? Suddenly going dark? It was scary to not be able to find or contact you.

I crossed my arms and stared at my shoes. All this time I'd been working at Mom's shop and getting myself to and from. Every week I delivered my sister and myself to two different homes, 89 percent on time.

Who didn't fall to pieces when Mom and Dad split? Me. Whose grades were better than decent? Mine. Who befriended that home-school kid who had no friends her age here (at first), even did homework for her (or at least with her)? Every week I ran Rex's and my laundry and mostly didn't leave a trail of balled-up socks. I made a habit of yes and no, please and thank you, sir and ma'am. Did anyone notice?

Top it off, I'd finally apologized to Gideon about candy snatching.

I didn't lock *myself* out of Soho, I muttered to the waiting adults. How come nobody's talkin' about that?

You said you'd be back in five, Stew said.

All you had to do is look out the door, I said. Mikey and me were right there!

My mother cut Stew off before he could respond.

She said, Don't explain yourself to him, Stewart. Jonas knows he should have waited until you returned or called immediately instead of hanging out with friends.

None of my friends were there, I said.

I didn't say how much downtown shoppers don't like me-type kids pressing our faces against the windows of closed shops. How quickly they notice, primed to speed-dial 911.

I DON'T CARE, Mom snapped, and even Rex went silent.

I thought we put this behavior behind us, she said. This isn't the only incident. I wish you would act a *little* more responsibly. Be as reliable as you seem to think you are.

A timer rang and Mom yanked out the amoeba-shaped pizza, slammed the pan on the stovetop. The pizza slid to the left and my sister's eyes widened. She let go of Stew's waist, where she'd been hanging, watching the situation tank, and retreated to outside the kitchen. I knew, if Mom made a move Rex didn't trust, she'd dart back in. That's how things went down back when our parents were regularly shouting at each other, before Dad moved out: Rex racing in and throwing out her hands. Stop it! she'd yell.

Stew pursed his lips and lifted his palms. You know, I was worried and I think I overreacted.

Because that's not what Mom is doing right now, I said under my breath as I folded my arms and leaned against the wall.

Of course she heard it.

Mom pointed. To your room.

I opened my mouth to grumble an apology, but she scooped up the spatula and smacked the countertop three times, loudly. Everything went dead silent.

I have had ENOUGH of this back talk! Mom said, hair sliding out of the clip she was using to hold it out of flour and cheese and stuff. That is NOT how we raised you! I don't want to see you again until you've figured out how you're supposed to speak to ADULTS.

I grabbed my bag, stomped past Rex in the living room, and took the stairs by twos. When I reached my room, I slammed my door hard enough to shake shingles off the roof.

C: Here's one with art.
If you can call it that.

—J

CANDY SNATCHING IN SIX EASY STEPS

I. I'm the wolf. I'm the storm
closing in. Running like
nobody's business as I rip
down broke-up sidewalks.
Flashing fast. Silent.
Moving like smoke.
Closing in.

II. World's a blur 'round me and my boys.
So black in our Fright Night gear: face
masks, hoodies, camo. Couldn't pick us
out with a flashlight.

III. We're ghosts when we run
up on them. Lil' kids screaming, squealing before we get
'em. Before we

i. shut
ii. them
iii. up.

IV. I'm the wolf. I'm the storm catching up.
I grab a sweatshirt. A costume rips. I grin
my ivories at the lil' freaked-out faces.
Growling, crazy scary with only eyeballs
and teeth showing. Mouth laughing,
I swing a brat around and
snatch the fat candy
sack.

V. I'm the wolf. I push a
kid and she falls or maybe
she runs. Kid's not dumb;
won't come back. Even if she
wants to,

    i. too late,
    ii. I'm gone.

VI. Running,

i. and laughing
ii. with my boys
iii. like boogeymen.

Chapter 12
Hits

I looked up at the light knock on my door. Dad, wearing a black cap with sparkly bits melting on top, stuck his head through the narrow space.

Yo. C'I come in? he rumbled in an extra-deep voice, imitating how he thinks teens sound.

I shrugged—not like I could say no. Not like I'd had any visitors, or any food, since seven thirty last night; jammed up in my room like that kid in a funky costume in the old picture book.

Dad's head disappeared, replaced by an arm and hand holding what looked like a paper-wrapped sandwich. He waggled it in my direction, and the scent of eggs and melted cheese wafted toward me. I peeled myself out of my desk chair and went over to pull the door wider. Then I moved to the side to let Dad pass. He stepped over a crumpled-up sweatshirt and a few spine-split books as more white stuff fell from his jacket.

First snow of the year, said Dad. It's light. Probably won't stick.

I peered out my window, where the sun was a slightly brighter blotch in a gray sky.

Mom called? I asked as I took the offered sandwich.

Dad tilted his head, squinted one eye.

About yesterday, I clarified while unwrapping the sandwich to reveal a perfect, round, toasted thing with cheese melted to the paper.

I took a big bite.

Whatever Mom had been going on about had maybe less to do with me than with Dad. They were often arguing about something or another.

Dad apparently didn't want to talk about Mom because he shrugged. Coming farther in, he peered at my desk.

Hard at work, huh? he said.

The desk lamp gave my room a quiet, sleepy feel. With Dad eyes, I inspected the scattered bits of my most recent zine effort: a full typed sheet, ripped squares of newspaper, the word "ran" in three sizes, liberated from Mom's magazines. No way was Dad learning anything from *that* mess.

So this is the Machine? Dad said, rubbing a finger across the top of the typewriter.

He hunched forward and rested all ten on the keys, pressed down QWERTY-style like they taught in school. His expression reminded me of the old dude with a towel over his shoulder who plays organ at the church on Christmas (the only time we go). My mollies bobbed dreamily in their tank as Dad's fingers moved on the keys like they were creating music. More like a bunch of shotguns sounding in a forest.

Man, that smell, Dad said. Grease and oil.

Coming out of it, he jerked his hands up. Wait. I didn't type over your homework?

I waved him off. That's scrap.

Want to tell me what happened last night? Dad asked out of nowhere.

Nothing to tell, I mumbled.

Mmm, replied Dad, Mom-style, and still not looking at me.

He went on, Your mom says she wakes up at night and you're at it with the typewriter. I don't know how you're not disturbing your sister.

Tigers couldn't wake her, I said.

The corners of Dad's eyes crinkled.

What I've got, he said, going back to the typewriter. You're not where you're expected to be; sometimes you're up in the middle of the night; you refuse to confide in your mom or me.

Dad paused, waggled his head, continued. You *did* walk in on me and your mom . . . can't be just that. Something's definitely up. If there was one, two things off, I could let it go.

Dad faced me fully, frowned.

Talk, Jonas, he said. Someone hurt you?

Looking at the remaining half of my sandwich, I shook my head. I should have explained, but I couldn't. Truman Abraham's son got good grades, listened to his mom, watched his kid sister. Tru's boy resembled him: a chip off the old block. Tru's boy wouldn't steal candy from babies or run down helpless girls. I swallowed, throat feeling stuffed though there was nothing in it.

You hurt somebody? Dad asked next.

No, I said too quick and too slow.

Dad gripped my chin, forcing me to look up into eyes like mine.

What aren't you saying? he asked.

That zine popped into my head: Consent for Every Body. Well, mine is a body and maybe I don't want to be grabbed.

Jerking my head away, I plopped the rest of the sandwich on my desk, knowing the grease would soak through and ruin whatever. I crossed my arms and stared down at my socks.

Jonas, Dad said, and this time, grabbed my elbow.

He lowered his voice. We're in your corner. Other people . . . they're not. Something happen at school? Maybe with one of your friends?

When I didn't say anything, his hand tightened. And tightened.

You're squeezing, I said.

Dad's voice rumbled like a subway train approaching. He said, I'm not asking you. This is not a choice. You need to come clean. NOW.

I said, I plead the Fifth.

He said, You see a court of law?

I said, So that means you can do whatever you want 'cause I'm a kid and you're grown up?

And I said, Right? Kids don't get a choice.

My elbow had gone a little numb by the time he let go. For show, I rubbed it, but really, didn't hurt more than his glare. More than knowing he'd learned that Tru's boy was *that* kind of kid. Somebody who hurt people.

After a long, silent moment, Dad left wordlessly. I rubbed at my chest as disappointment swelled. Tried to convince myself: better this way.

* * *

After that winner of a morning, I found myself in the hall at school, surveying kids getting themselves to class. The energy was pretty high since it was the half day before Thanksgiving, but I felt in a different place from everyone else. Kinda nervous, maybe.

I asked myself, Do this? Or don't?

Thumbs rubbing the scratchy fabric under my backpack straps, I considered the two typed notes in my pants pocket. One for Gideon (`text me,` with my phone number). Even if it turned out Mikey was behind the other notes, Halloween sat center in the whirling winds of trouble.

The other note, weirdly, had been harder to write.

The hall started to clear for the next class. Kids calling out. Lockers shrilling and shuddering when they banged closed.

Do it? Don't?

Since our last names are alphabet-opposite, Gideon's locker was far from mine. Charity O'Dell, it turned out, was good for nothing, but Ton O' Braids had the scoop about Gideon's locker's location since she's an office volunteer. One text to Darius was all it took for her to snoop before school started this morning. (DD claims she's got a thing for Nancy Drew, whoever that is.)

Do it? Don't?

My message to Gideon wasn't exactly a mystery. The other one, though . . . how likely was it they wouldn't know I was behind it?

I stuffed the note in my pocket, and stepped out of the shadow.

Dad always says there's a time to move forward and a time to step back. *Up to you to decide which, when.*

Do it. Moving fast, I rushed down the line of lockers and poked the slip of paper through the orange slats of a top locker. A second note went into a locker I knew, a gray one near my science room.

Keep stepping back, fall off a cliff. Right?

* * *

What'd you do? a kid asked as I gathered my stuff together in my last class before early release.

What? I blinked at him.

Wasn't anyone I usually talked to. I glanced around but everything else was normal . . . enough.

The kid watched me curiously as I shrugged on my backpack, silent the whole while.

My feet moved on their own toward the door. The hallway sounded normal: voices, shouts, lockers swinging open and shut. I directed myself to homeroom to wait for the bell, already planning how I'd take Rex to C.'s instead of going home, continue avoiding the parents. (Maybe avoid Stew, too?)

I nearly missed the message when my sneakers passed over: JONAS DID IT. Written in sparkly pink marker, two feet tall, right there on the floor.

First thought: Did what?

My second thought: Run.

Buses hadn't been called, walkers were to wait in their assigned areas, but who could bother with that at a time like this? Way at the end of the hall, steps led down to the first-floor main entrance where wide green doors were just waitin' for kids to shove through. Usually, near those doors, VP or the principal monitored the dismissal situation using clipboards and buzzing walkie-talkies.

Back door, then.

I turned right on top of my name. A tiny hope bloomed, an option I hadn't considered. Taking a quick knee, I rubbed two fingers over the giant "Jo." Smudge of color stuck to my fingers, but otherwise the letters didn't budge.

My third thought: Gideon.

The note I'd left in her locker said **text me**, not *spray-paint my name across Upper School*. The Gideon I'd seen in North River, the one who stared a lot with her big deer eyes but said little, didn't seem likely to snag a hall pass to do THIS.

On the other hand. If it *was* Gideon, I needed to turn her in to VP Hong STAT. The situation called for a running toward, not a running away. Locate VP. Clear my name.

I spun and started toward her second-floor office, but what I saw next stopped me again. Tied to lockers, several colorful balloons bobbed. I could easily read the same three handwritten words: JONAS DID IT.

Kids fast-walked or wandered past, many giving the balloons interested or confused glances, a few goggling at me, maybe waiting for the punch line. For the funny to start.

Something started. It was my heart, going *THUMPTHUMP-THUMP*.

Something else started. It was my mind leaping and tumbling and spinning, trying to figure out how somebody had time to do graffiti AND blow up some actual floating balloons, write my name on 'em—all before twelve noon. Did he skip all his classes today? She hide out under the stairs with a Sharpie and a balloon tank? Where did they even GET a balloon tank?

Sweat rolled down my armpits as I grabbed the string of the first balloon and yanked. As I moved to retrieve the next one, I tucked the first beneath my jacket, pulled house keys from my pocket, and jammed them into the soft rubber. The *pop!* wasn't very muffled.

I snatched up the final five balloons and killed them dead in the nearby stairwell. Then I joined the small crowd walking down to floor one, ignoring every instance of anybody speaking my name since not once was anyone talking TO me. More like about me.

Kids walked by as I peered around the doorjamb and spotted a single yellow balloon that seemed low on helium, bobbing sadly toward the floor. Three more balloons, here and there, in red and orange and green.

JONAS DID IT JONAS DID IT JONAS DID IT

No chance I'd get them down and busted before the teachers caught wind. How hadn't they already spotted them?

Yeah. The only choice left to me now was to run for it. (Hobo life, I thought, here I come.) The door was open and I could make out the yellow of a few buses idling. I was sure I could truck faster than any flabby teacher.

Out of nowhere, a voice piped up: What?

I leaped half out of my skin.

One of her buns was limp and falling, half spun out. I grabbed her arm. This was the first time we'd gotten close enough to touch since Halloween.

Gideon's eyes were dark under the shadow of the stairs. She shook me off and pointed into the hallway, mouthing, Not me.

Should have been more of a relief.

BOP! We both jumped.

BOPBOPBOP!

Near the stairwell exit, but not so close that I could reach Mikey or Charity O'Dell or her goons with ease. Words exploded, and the five of them stood in the bright-lit hall, making it happen. Stabbing with pushpins and keys, their faces grinning like jack-o'-lanterns but crazier, scarier. Fearless before VP's sharp eyes, before her two-finger whistle and one-button dial to suspension.

JONAS DID IT.

JONAS DID IT.

JONAS DID IT.

A couple of kids screamed and things dropped, backpacks and books and pens. People scattered.

With my own eyes, I watched Mikey and friends dropping balloon carcasses. *Friends.* Okay, but not Double D, not Aaron, and not me. Different friends. Charity's girls flanked them, and one shrank, giggling, into a classroom doorway with a pink metal tank. Helium, like for kids' birthday parties, like for fun and maybe an Ultimate Prank where a kid tries to one-up and embarrass his buddy, his FRIEND, nudging him toward trouble but nothing serious. Right?

Joooo—nas! Charity cupped her hands around her mouth like her big ol' pipes needed any extra help. What. Did. You. DO?

Mikey doubled over. I saw he was shaking, holding himself. I ran over, leaving Gideon to the safety of shadows. When I reached his side, Mikey straightened, howling with laughter, and pointed at me.

That, I told myself, is your boy.

Sound burst in a wave, yelling girl voices and shoes slapping down the hall. At least the popping had stopped. I heard teacher voices. Somebody grabbed my sweatshirt, but two twists and I was free, closing in with my hand up to slap Mikey five. Like, good one.

Like, you got me, man.

Mikey raised his hand, too, but mine flew by and made cracking-contact with his face. In the movies, dudes fall if you hit 'em hard enough; they go right out. In real life, when I shut my fist and hit a second time, something hard over Mikey's left eye met my knuckles like a wall. He grabbed me around the middle and we went over. My knees came up to protect and I rolled us, got him by the end of the braids that had fuzzed out since his sister last did 'em.

I didn't care anymore WHO left those dumb notes, who scrawled my name in pink, who found time to blow up balloons and smear my name, who wanted Halloween to roar up and swallow me.

Jonas did it? Sure. I was doing IT right now.

I paid Mikey back.

DO NOT SHARE WITH C.

THIS IS HOW IT HAPPENED

How it happened: Mikey wanted to go after a group of upper-school girls.

We were headed home. Aaron's grandma called, so he had already left on his skateboard. Wasn't no one expecting me: Rex at a party, Mom with friends, Dad who knew where?

Mikey said, They're just girls.

I wasn't down. Maybe they wouldn't recognize us, but we already had TONS of candy. Also, the bigger the kid you snatch from, the more work.

Darius said, You comin'?

I went. They're my boys.

And easy, right? Chase 'em, catch 'em, grab the candy. But somebody's sneaker scuffed, and the girls heard.

A pineapple stopped under a streetlight. The other girls stood in shadow. Four together, sniffing the air.

I slowed. Kids knew to watch for us, so I was thinking: Maybe not. Then Mikey and Darius jumped through the bushes.

WHOOP WHOOP WHOOP!

Girls started running. Screaming. A plastic bucket cracked
against the sidewalk. Candy flew out, shooting across the
ground like stars.

My heart: thumpthumpTHUMP.

Away ran the pineapple, away ran Dorothy from The Wizard
of Oz, a cat, and something that looked like what the laundry
puked up. That last girl was fast. I'm quicker than any of
the boys, so I followed. Thought it'd be funny to nab a
running pile of socks.

It wasn't.

Chapter 13
MISSES

Mom pulled into our driveway and cut the engine. Then she sat there, both hands on the wheel. Holding a mostly warm ice pack to my cheek, I stared down at fish crackers that had beached themselves in a rainbow around Rex's booster seat.

We waited, listening to the *clickticktick* of the engine cooling. Finally, Dad's Miata rolled up behind us.

Mom's eyes flashed in the rearview mirror.

Stay, she commanded, and opened her door.

My parents' shadows met at the side of the car. My mother's voice rose and her finger jabbed. Dad was a rumble I could barely hear till he ran out of his "magic words won at college" (Mom's saying), and then his voice barked and snapped. Soon enough he stalked away, but just to the edge of the drive, where he faced the street and took a giant breath that made his shoulders rise.

I unbuckled my seat belt, slid down, and pulled my knees up to press against the seat in front of me. This was the first time I was in it for fighting since lower school. I could barely remember that far back, but I know I didn't get suspended 'cause I was basically a baby. I bet Mom yelled, Dad took away the TV and game privileges, and my teachers worked up a plan for "increased impulse control."

My impulses weren't the problem. Mikey had started this whole thing. Who knew why?

I pulled the ice pack from my face and dropped it on the seat beside me, reaching for the door handle. Opened the door and caught sight of Mom, both her hands gesturing wildly.

If you knew something was off, why'd you let him go? she demanded. Why didn't you TELL me? I thought we were co-parenting—

Olivia, interrupted Dad from the curb, I'm supposed to pull him from school on a hunch? What was I going to do? I was so swamped last night, I had to leave the kids with you—I know you weren't pleased about that. Then I had a very sensitive meeting today with a client, and not the kind you can drag your kid to, stick him in a corner with a laptop.

Tru, you could have said! Her head was shaking back and forth, and she crossed her arms. I find out you've been seeing this . . . *off* behavior? Why didn't you TELL me?

Olivia, Dad said again, and tilted his head at where I peered around the door.

Mom pinned me with her eyes. What did I say, child? Stay in the car.

At the same time, Dad said, Go in the house.

I froze. Up on the electric wires, birds spied us. In the trees up and down the street, nosy squirrels watched. In the sky, satellites tracked us, three red-and-orange heat signatures on blue-green cool pavement. Or maybe a Google Street View car was driving past, capturing us so we'd appear, frozen, in search engine results next month. Everybody watching. Everyone seeing what we'd become.

It's just me, I announced, 'cause I wasn't sure what else to say.

I mean, I tried again but stopped when Mom's eyes narrowed.

She said, I don't want to hear a word out of your mouth right now.

Dad said, Oh. That's perfect. Boy hasn't let us in for weeks, and you're here slamming the door.

They faced off again.

Mom snapped, Why do you do this? Contradict me?

Dad said, This isn't about you, O. Let's at least agree to keep to the real issue.

Feeling eyes on me (but not my parents' eyes, since theirs were on each other), I started to inch away.

Mom: Yes. Why don't you INFORM me of the real issue? Because nothing I have to say, nothing I add has any value in your eyes—

Dad: You know what? I'm sick of this. Stop playing the martyr—

Mom: Oh BS, Truman. You are so FULL of it.

Dad (taking a step back, dragging his hands over his face): We need to stop making a scene in the damn driveway. Let's you and me go somewhere neutral to talk.

Mom: We have forty minutes before I need to pick Roxanne up. Also? (pointing to me without looking) Our son? Got in a brawl with his friend at school and there's some mysterious thing he *did* that we don't know about, and he's now a statistic, suspended. You want to leave him *alone*?

Dad (barely glancing my way): Jonas. Go in the house.

I did.

You made this happen, I told myself. You wanted no more back-and-forth, because it's too hard for Rex, for them, for you. Hanging on hurts worse than letting go.

Moving farther into the house, I heard the sharp crack of a slamming car door, an engine starting up. One car stayed, the other drove away.

Biting my lip, swollen from the fight, I said aloud to no one, I did that, too.

It was true.

It's all true. Jonas did it.

* * *

I'd expected more yelling, but there was mostly silence. Despite arguing about it, my parents left me on my own. At around six, Darius started blowing up my phone with texts. Got some from Aaron, even from Ton. Didn't read a single one.

Eventually, I heard Rex and Mom enter the house. No Dad. No one appeared in my room, looking mad or nosy or disappointed. Doors opened, closed. Sun dipped. The laptop was with Mom and I wanted to be anywhere *but*, so I couldn't check Friendspace or Chatter to see what kids were saying about the fight, such as:

• Who won before Dr. Adeyemo peeled us apart? (me)

• Who said what behind VP Hong's office door? (VP from a tall-backed super-villain chair asked me questions, then Mikey, next Charity and kids who'd been in the hall and seen.)

• What happened when Mikey's sister arrived after driving hours in midday traffic from Newark? (Her anger burned him to a crisp?)

Right before six, VP Hong called to check in. It was strange for a number of reasons. First, VP sounds like a lil' kid over the phone. Second, she wasn't looking to talk to my parents so much as with me. Third, she told me that Mikey had asked to circle up, and when I said what's the point since we're suspended anyway, VP went on for a bit about "opportunities to learn from one another" and "clearing the air."

Yeah. Okay. I'd only done a mediation circle once before. Mikey had gotten me and DD in it with VP over a trick that made a kid faint. (He was fine!) School had started doing these circles when my class hit the upper grades, and at first, all the kids were excited because we thought that meant detentions would go away. Nope. What it really meant was that some kids told the truth, others lied or tried to, a few cried, and everybody left feeling weirded out 'cause now folks knew too much about their secrets—and then had ISS or detention anyway.

VP said, Jonas, is there anyone you want to accompany you?

I said, What, like a hype man?

She said, Members of the school community who you feel have your back.

Uh. Wasn't that the main issue? My boys were supposed to be my crew. Instead one tried to frame me, and what help were the other two? None.

Me: How many will Mikey have?

VP: He's reached out to one or two people.

Me: I'll bring three.

VP: Wonderful. If you're thinking of a teacher or school staff, I'm happy to help make that connection. I believe you're new to this process. Although all upper-school students participate in the circles as part of the advisory period, this will be a little different. Do you have any questions?

Me: Not really.

VP: One other thing. When Mrs. White heard what happened on Wednesday, she wanted to help. That's great because she's trained to facilitate. Are you okay with having her there?

And to think I'd almost told Mrs. White about Gideon and candy snatching during school community service. Instead, we had a typewriter nerd-out. If anyone, Mrs. White is the one person I could trust not to freak out and hate me forever. Also, probably Dr. Adeyemo.

Me: Sure.

VP: Thank you, Jonas. Monday morning, then, eight a.m. sharp in the library.

* * *

The moon outside my window bloomed into a half circle. I heard Rex loudly calling for Mom.

Still no Dad. Good or bad?

At eight, Rex appeared holding a plate with two slices of bread pasted together with probably half an inch of peanut butter.

Made you dinner, she said as she flopped bonelessly next to me where I was working on the floor.

Holding the sandwich out, she swiveled her head like an owl.

What you looking so hard for? I asked, accepting the choke sandwich. Thanks.

She checked under the bed skirt.

Rex, I warned as I peeled the bread back to see how much peanut butter I was gonna have to contend with.

Where'd all the stuff go? she asked. Like, the clothes and the papers and the books?

I rolled my eyes. I clean. Sometimes. Mom didn't cook?

Rex shrugged. Leftovers. I know you don't like eggplant.

Neither do you, I reminded her.

I like it okay, she said, and reached hot fingers to poke my cheek.

Does it hurt? she asked.

No, I lied. And you definitely do NOT like eggplant.

Mikey did that? Rex touched her own face, eyes scrunching.

None of your business, I said, and took a big enough bite to not be able to talk anymore.

Later, when I couldn't fall sleep, I blearily considered the typewriter. Rescued a towel from my hamper and wrapped it around the base to muffle the sound (so stop complaining, MOM). Before I started up, I read what Dad had typed out.

```
it was a dark and stormy night. we were babes
in college, and you babies weren't born yet. up
late, writing. out cold in class. tonight, love,
what's your heart's delight
```

A sorta poem. I scrolled to a fresh position and put my fingers to the keys. Nothing. Tried getting some letters down, complete nonword nonsense, but everything stopped again; two words in, five words in. I spied Robin's zines poking out of a bin at the edge of my desk. There were four or so I hadn't read, or given to C. as promised.

I tugged them out and spread myself across my bed. Disappeared into black-and-white and two-color; into cursive that had to be decoded like a treasure map; into drawings, some goofy and others that made me wish I was a quarter as good; a poem so long I gave up before the end; and two comics, one with chunky art like Aaron's manga with the beefy dudes whose hair turns blond when they power up, the other a story comic with funny drawings of a family living in the East Village.

The zines showed life different from books I read for school. After I closed the last one, I had a better idea of what C. had been trying to tell me. Passing my eyes over a funny kind of treasure spread across my bed: other worlds, wild/sad/funny stories, all written by no one exactly like me or like C. Her page would totally fit. Mine might, too.

Back at my desk, I placed my fingers on the keys and I let my sleepy mind leap.

C: Forget the others.
Use this. —J

REASONS WHY MIKEY SUCKS

People should know that what happened in October wasn't completely my fault.

Here's why:

i. That girl shouldn't have broke off from the group

ii. When I caught her, it wasn't cool that she tried to knee me in the junk

    -Mikey tries that all the time when we goof around; I'm an expert blocker

    -Pisses me off

iii. Head-butting don't work unless you know how to do it

iv. It's just candy

    -Candy is CHEAP

    -Just. Get. More.

It's mostly Mikey's fault. He's the one who started us snatching, and it was his idea to go after those girls. I mean: Aaron had gone home / we'd collected enough candy / folks were ready to leave.

You're wondering why I went
along when I knew
it was dumb?

v. Wasn't the candy

vi. Wasn't because Mikey
did peer-pressure juju

vii. Didn't feel sorry for
Darius always doing what Mikey
says 'cause he can't say no

Look. The situation was:

viii. The girls ran and we HAD to follow.
We were a pack of wolves, shoulder to shoulder

ix. Wolves chase deer; it's proven

x. Deer stay together, then they break off;
wolves stay together and then THEY break off

xi. One deer leaped. This wolf followed

xii. It didn't need to be that big a deal

Chapter 14

SUNK

Friday morning, Darius texted: Where are you today? Dungeon?

Glancing over my shoulder at Mom and Rex entering an animal camouflage exhibit, I wandered away so I could respond in peace.

Me: Nope. Liberty Science Center

Darius: Jersey City? Oh. Are you visiting family for Thanksgiving?

Me: That was canceled. I'm too naughty. Grinch came and took it away

Darius: Wrong holiday

Darius: Really? No turkey?

Me: My parents were kinda distracted

And anyway, I thought, nobody felt like cooking. I fried up triple-decker grilled cheese sandwiches for Rex and me and put a Disney marathon on down in the den, while Mom hid in her bedroom, complaining for hours on the phone to Aunt Demi.

Darius: Gracie said her friend's sister caught the whole fight on her phone and had uploaded it to Chatter but somehow VP found out and CALLED Gracie's friend's sister's house and made her take it down!

Me: We coulda been famous

Darius: Infamous

Darius: VP's a ninja

I didn't get that, but D went on: I heard Mikey got ISS. Plus he has to talk to school psych

Me: Always said he was nuts

Darius: I heard you'll be meeting with her too

Me: Who says

Darius: I can't believe you get into a fight at school and your parents take you to a museum

Me: Don't forget they deleted Thanksgiving

I turned to follow their progress through the exhibit, watching them lean over something in an open-top glass tank, heads close. Rex pointed. Mom laughed. Fuzzy yellow things bopped around— baby chicks? I tried not to feel like I'd been transported to the Twilight Zone.

Darius: I just heard from Mikey he's in it big. His MOM called!!!!

Me (wondering, How's it bad if somebody's mother calls? Especially if that mother is in prison? Seems like a good thing?):

Me: Serves him right

Great clouds of visitors drifted between me and my family, but the sounds weren't like school hallways between class. There was a calm buzz to the place, with once-in-a-while announcements about lightning shows or people who should go to the information desk because other people were waiting.

Darius: You didn't have to hit him like that

Me: Are you kidding? He's a putz. He tried to rat me out to the whole school

Darius: About what, anyway?? Halloween?

Me: Always knew those notes were from him

Darius: ?!

Darius: I never got why you think he would do that

Me: Have you MET Mikey?

Me: [. . .]

Me: Did you help??

Darius: No!

Me: You only used one "!"

Darius: [. . .]

Me: [. . .]

Darius: Look can you be mad at him for just a little while and not forever? Because that would suck

Rex calling my name prompted me to slide the phone into my sweatshirt pocket and follow her and my mom to yet another science thingy I wouldn't pay a lick of attention to.

How's it going, Baby Bear? Mom asked, slipping an arm over my shoulder.

Her hair was pulled into a bun, and she looked strange without earrings and lipstick outside the house.

We going to be here how long? I asked, the smell of old wood and carpets hitting me as we entered a room devoted to ancient, dust-covered arithmetic.

I sneezed several times.

Why? Mom asked, palm passing over my forehead. Feeling okay?

I'm fine, I muttered as I rubbed my nose. All this smelly old wood.

Mom's hand accidentally brushed the bruise on my cheek before dropping to my shoulder. I jumped a little and wriggled away. She frowned.

The museum is Rex's choice, Mom said. You haven't told me what you want to do. Better come up with something soon. Restrictions begin at midnight, and then you'll never see daylight outside of school and home again.

Ha ha, I muttered.

Mom raised an eyebrow. Mmm.

I changed the subject. Are you gonna go to Soho Stationery later to see how Stew did with the Black Friday sale?

Mom shook her head. He's been keeping me in the loop by text. It was busy, but nothing he couldn't handle, especially with a few teens helping out. I do plan to spend most of tomorrow at the shop, though. How about seeing a movie tonight? Or, you know, you don't have to hang with your sister and me. Dad's free, too.

Why aren't you mad at me? I asked.

It was spooky, all the not-hollering, the no-punishment, and the eerie-niceness.

She inspected me as we trailed along behind Rex. Eventually Mom spoke, crossing her arms and leaning against a display.

She said, Your dad and I talked. He says, since you . . . saw us together at his place, you've been upset. Won't give him the time of day. Sound familiar?

Mom waited, but I didn't respond, so she continued. Then there's this graffiti thing at school, something Mikey wrote? And balloons! That boy. Anything to add?

Me:

Mom nodded and said, There you go. Dad says we've lost your trust—you used to tell us things. I say you're twelve—that's one year away from being a full-fledged pain in the butt. We've given you a lot of freedom because you make excellent grades and you work hard at Soho, take care of your sister. Maybe too much freedom. What's changed? Your dad and I don't have a clue—I mean beyond our, uh, dynamic, which admittedly can be a lot to take.

What's changed? I looked at the ceiling, so far above us, so concrete and boring you'd never notice it in a million years. Blinked a few times, making sure things were dry around the eyeballs while I cleared my throat carefully, low so she wouldn't hear.

Nothing's changed, I muttered.

Mom pulled her lips to one side. Her eyes said: lies. Then she banked right into a walled-off space where Rex had disappeared to stuff her brain with Aztec math or whatever.

My phone buzzed.

Darius: Heads up. Word on the street is VP called Gideon's parents after your and Mikey's fight last Wednesday

Me: What street is that

Darius: Chatter. I'm on a private channel with Gracie and some other kids. VP Hong and the lower school VP tag-teamed 'cause it's so many of Charity's girls in trouble. I guess VP Hong didn't have time to call everybody herself before the holiday. At least that's what I heard

Me: . . .

Darius: Couple girls got caught trying to turn off the helium tank, it was leaking gas everywhere

Darius: I think it's weird school called Gideon's people, tho. She wasn't even there

Me: Yeah she was. In the stairwell

Darius: Keep you updated. Gracie figures she'll get more deets on Monday

So will I, I thought. Firsthand.

I pocketed my phone. Rex came skipping from the arithmetic exhibit and propped herself against me where I held up the wall near a set of overwhelmed old aunties.

Kid said, Hey.

I said, Horses.

She giggled on cue. I grinned at her big-headed cuteness and felt some funk fall away. At the end of a long, awful week, I'd gotten one thing right.

One thing, I told myself. It's a start.

*   *   *

Mom appearing in my room before bed was surprising, especially after hours together at the Science Center and at Playland Beach Arcade. We were all surprised that place was open so late in the fall. I shot enough baskets at NBA Hoop Shoot to win tickets to trade for two plastic spider rings (one for Rex, one for Mom) and a rubber popper toy (Mikey'd love that, not that he'd ever get it).

This when freedom officially ends? I asked, rolling onto my back like an otter with her phone pressed to my front.

You can have an hour more, Mom said. But now IS when you give me back my phone.

It's suspiciously clean in here, she added under her breath.

I'm a neat person, I said.

She said, Mmm. Hand over the phone. Thirty seconds or I permanently delete Veggie Pirates.

Harsh! I said, tossing the phone, which she caught. The pirates wouldn't plague you if I had a real phone like everybody else.

Mom snorted. You're sassing me about reclaiming my phone, which I pay for. After I spent the day carting you and Roxanne around, plying you with treats—which is something, for the record, your dad suggested. Personally, I voted for the throw-away-the-keys approach.

Hey, I said. I won you a spider ring.

She laughed.

Point, I thought, smiling.

Mom wandered to my desk. Books and papers were sorted into stacks, but my art materials were still out. The mollies observed her from their tank as she eyed the pink typewriter wrapped in its towel cozy.

This thing, she said. Who knew you'd get so into it? Waking me up at night . . .

Mom's hand landed on a my stack of zine materials. I didn't think much of it; my best zine pages and C.'s were hidden under the bed, far from prying eyes (turns out bed skirts are useful).

Mom said. Is this one of—? Jonas! You've been cutting up *Yoga Journal*?

Uh-oh. Standing, I was frozen in place by her glare. Mom snatched up the open magazine.

She said, This is the CURRENT issue! Chiiiild.

Then she said, in a different voice, What IS this?

I asked, What's what?

She lifted one of Robin's zines that I had been skimming earlier, before the call of Veggie Pirates became too great. She brought the page closer to her face. Mom's eyes widened and then narrowed. That zine, she tucked beneath her arm.

I asked you a question, Mom said. What are these and where did you get them?

They're zines, I said. Like, short for magazines? People make 'em. And, uh, North River Books. Robin said I should pass them to C.

To do what with? Mom asked.

For ideas? I said. Me and C. are working on one together?

Mom tilted her head in that spooky way she does sometimes, eyes boring into me. Her expression said many things, but mostly: Are You Out of Your Mind? She held one zine open, showing a drawing of a woman with no clothes. Oh, right. That.

Mom said, Robin gave you materials that are . . . inappropriate for someone your age?

I groaned, Mom, come on! Robin McCormick wouldn't give me something bad.

So you haven't read this? Mom shook the page so hard I was surprised the naked lady didn't fall out on the floor.

I guess I looked at them a little, I lied.

Mom removed the one from beneath her arm and read aloud the title: A Young Person's Guide to Consent for Every Body. I'm confiscating these to review. *Maybe* you'll get them back.

Pressing the collection of zines against her face, she moaned, How much can ONE boy get into in ONE week?

I crossed my arms. Not fair. You come into my room and start going through my stuff!

She yanked down the zines and glared. Who pays for this room?

Those were a gift! I said.

Jonas— Mom's voice deepened with aggravation, only to be interrupted by Rex in the doorway.

Mom? she said.

Kid zipped in and stood between us, facing our mother down. For some reason, that made me feel . . . not good.

Rex, it's fine, Mom said impatiently. To me, she announced, Your father and I need to review ALL of these.

Her eyes searched out hidey-holes. In the trash, I'd stuffed several rejected attempts. Before I questioned the wisdom, I darted past Rex and intercepted, lifting the can from the floor.

Mom's expression clouded. Instead of upset, she seemed, well . . .

I retreated from reach before the storm crashed down.

* * *

Which is how Rex and I ended up at Dad's.

Dad showed up ten minutes after my sister called him from the emergencies-only landline in the kitchen. He didn't enter the house, but spoke quietly with Mom with his car window rolled down, taking in the cold night air and a short stack of zines. He set up the pull-out couch like usual and didn't ban Rex or me from using twenty-first-century technology in bed, which was my plan now.

I padded down the metal spiral staircase and unearthed Dad's tablet from beneath folders on the dining table. Dad was snoring nearby, face covered by a blanket with the top of his head sticking out, fade looking as mussed as it'd ever get.

I brought the tablet upstairs and got to work wasting Veggie Pirates with the sound turned off. Carrots and cukes fell every which way as I swiped and tapped. My reflection in the fingerprint-smudged screen reminded me that my hair needed a trim and . . . were those bags under my eyes?

I paused the game, tapped the camera app. Yup. Bags. I patted one to see how deep it went, sighed, flopped over backward. Ran both hands down my face. *Should try to sleep.* Soon as I closed my eyes, though, the blender that was my brain whirled to life, and pretty much everyone I'd spoken to or ignored or wished I could approach collided, each screeching to be heard over the other. Each time, my eyes snapped open without permission.

Sighing, I rolled onto my side and slid the tablet under a pillow. House wasn't silent; I heard the heat click on and off and the murmur of a TV next door. Outside, cars occasionally swooshed past and I counted them. Then I counted what I could see of the thick books on the wooden shelf across from the bed.

Next I knew, I was jerking awake as my head rolled off the pillow. My heart felt like it was clawing to escape my chest, and I sucked in a breath and some spit, too, which made me hack. I jumped when a hand landed on my neck, and tried to turn to face the bedroom door, but it was like someone had grabbed both ends of a hammock and twirled me—I was that caught up.

You were shouting in your sleep, said Dad in a groggy voice.

He started pulling at the sheets. Here. Let's get you . . . untangled.

I worked from within, and he plucked and tugged, and between the two of us we freed my limbs. I sat up, using the sides of my thumbs to rub water out of my eyes. For one horrified moment, I thought: *tears*. But no. Sweat.

Dad stood, clicked on a lamp, and grabbed the edge of my blanket. He lifted it, letting it fly. As the softness *flumped* onto my legs, I remembered how my parents used to tuck Rex and me in. They'd flap the blankets again and again, sometimes both of them getting into the act at once, trying to outdo each other. Couple times I took the edge of a blanket in the eye, but I never asked them to stop. Sometimes I'd help them do it to Rex, and she'd giggle and shriek.

Your T-shirt is soaked, Dad said as he walked over to his dresser to get a replacement.

It's okay, I told him, but he tossed me one of his and waited while I made the swap—soft, warm, worn through.

Then he tossed my sweaty shirt toward his overflowing hamper and squatted beside the bed. Dad clicked off the lamp. Except for the shine of his eyes, he was hard to see.

Talk about it? he asked.

I shook my head.

Dad nodded. When you're ready, then.

I wondered, When will I be ready?

I thought, Never.

I offered, I'm okay. It's fine.

Dad snorted softly. Little man, I don't think a single thing is fine.

I pictured him behind the wheel in his spotless Miata, hoisting his spoon over a sweet-smelling Italian ice; refereeing between Rex and me at the supermarket, wearing his straight-from-work black and grays; standing rigidly at the edge of the driveway, face in shadow, hidden.

We're doing our best, Dad added, almost like an apology.

I didn't see Dad reaching toward me, so I flinched when his hand suddenly appeared. He made a low sound before continuing on his path to lift a corner of my pillow and drag out the tablet.

Not so soft, he commented without mentioning how jumpy I was. This thing makes a bad second pillow.

Dad pressed the on button and quietly viewed my paused game. Swiping with his thumb, he set it in motion. I rolled onto my side and Dad settled cross-legged with his back against the bed, where I could watch over his shoulder while he lost the level, bombed ALL my levels. Sank the game.

Chapter 15

RESCUE

What? I said while carefully manning a glue stick. You think I'm just . . . trouble all the time?

C.'s blue eyes flicked up. She smiled.

Draped in two of Tío's flannel shirts, she'd been working on her planet project and then switched to zine stuff while I made another sorry attempt at art and froze my butt off. The door between the porch and the rest of the house was partly open to let in pathetic little wisps of warm air, but mostly we got Rodrigo's blasting reggaeton. C. had that bluesy-rock band on, Styrofoam Rockets, making the tinny Bluetooth speaker buzz with bass.

Shouldn't complain—I was lucky to be here, since I was technically on restriction and not supposed to do anything remotely fun or interesting for the rest of the month and most of December. If Rex and I hadn't gotten banished to Dad's, I'd probably be alone in my bedroom, not even my phone for company, bouncing balled socks against the ceiling. Also helped that Mom was distracted with all the Small Business Saturday stuff.

Glad you have such a high opinion of me, I told C.

Well, she said. I have read your zine pages.

I stilled. That supposed to mean?

Trouble knows trouble. C. shrugged.

Behind her, planets were scattered around like a papier-mâché Milky Way, each in a swirl of painted-up newspapers, like some intergalactic chicken had laid the solar system. Nearby the windows showed more early-season snow coming down. It was kind of hard to believe, only a few weeks ago, my boys and me beat the pavement in shorts and hoodies, sleeves pushed up to our elbows.

Aha, C. spoke to the paper she'd been folding. She took metal scissors and started to snip. After a bit, handed me what looked like a tiny book. I took it and flipped the blank pages.

This is a dummy, she said. It's an example of what we're making.

Isn't it small? I asked, thinking about what I'd written (and balled up) so far. *I could fill this.* Not that I wanted to.

C. said, We could make mini-zines.

Handing the book back, I switched topics, asking, Do the planets have the same names in Chile as they do here?

C. pointed out each lumpy stellar body: Mercurio, Venus, Tierra, Marte, Júpiter, Saturno, Urano, Neptuno, Plutón.

Urano, I repeated. I *guess* that's an improvement.

Her face split as she laughed, smacking her knee. I grinned, wondering how I might inspire that again. Her laptop interrupted: *bleep-bloop.*

Who that? I asked. You don't have any other friends.

She made a face. I got pololos all over the world.

Creaky ol' librarians? I teased.

Sliding my glue-sticked masterpiece to the side, I crawled closer to C., trying to make out the face on her screen. She turned it away, but who escapes Jonas if I don't want 'em to? Nobody.

Hey! C. shouted as I distracted her with one waving arm and then used the other to snag the laptop screen, lift it out of her grip.

I got an eyeful: dark-haired boy, older than either of us, with face shaded by the bill of a baseball cap and a smirk I instantly hated. Behind his fat head, the sky was a bright, smooth blue. Red rooftops on short, blocky brick houses that stretched into the distance. Definitely not New Jersey.

Holding the laptop out of reach, I said, mostly to myself, Who's this schmo?

C. wrested her laptop back and pushed me hard enough to make me tumble.

She informed me, No one you need to know about.

True. Maybe C. had friends everywhere. What was it to me?

I resumed my cutting and pasting, mind cycling through images of Mikey and Charity, Darius and Gracie, Aaron and, well, many seventh-grade girls. Back before Halloween, I saw the boys looking at those girls more. Told myself, fine, let 'em. What was it hurting, 'sides me having to listen to dumb chatter?

Your mom know? I asked C., curious.

C. rolled her eyes. About what? Juan-Rupert is in Munich. It's not like we're . . . doing it.

My mouth dropped open. C. giggled and this time I didn't like the sound. You don't know what it means? It means sex. S-E-X—

I had the urge to throw something, but if C. came after me, we'd steamroll the planets and my zine, and then I'd be in another fight with another friend.

Instead, I raised my voice. Cut it OUT. Stop acting weird!

Footsteps. The volume on the reggaeton leaped as Tío Rodrigo appeared in the doorway. His usually friendly expression absent, he reached down and tugged C. up by the arm.

What has gotten into you two? he demanded, looking between us.

C.'s eyes flared and her mouth opened like she was gonna yell, but Tío ducked to speak speed-Spanish that I couldn't follow even the edges of, calling her revoltosa, and tugging at the sleeve of her shirt as he emphasized every word. She bowed her head, nodding.

Tío (who smelled *delicious*, like onions and toasted bread) got a hand on my wrist, too, drawing me up.

He asked, Is there something you want to tell Concepción, Jonas?

What? I said. She started it!

Tío frowned and gave my arm a shake.

Okay, okay. I rolled my eyes. *Sorry.*

¿Sí pués? he prompted, adding, Try again, without the eyes.

When I glared across at C., the corner of her mouth tugged once, twice.

My brain caught on. Instead of struggling to stay calm, I fought the urge to laugh. *What're we, five?*

Why? I said. 'Cause C. is a MUCH better friend than . . . other kids I know.

C.'s wiggling mouth stilled. Her head tilted. A smile rose in her eyes.

Fantástico, Tío told us. Now, go away. Walk it off so I can finish writing in peace.

* * *

Marine Park, which was about ten minutes walking from C.'s place, was mostly empty. Too cold for foolishness down by the water, so C. and me perched side by side on the back of a bench with our sneakers on the seat. We were as close to the river as we could get without suffering icy sprays brought in by the wind. I alternated between feeling annoyed at C. for attacking me and finding the whole episode incredibly funny. C. seemed to feel the same; a smile occasionally visited her face while we took ourselves out of Tío's hair. Probably why we were friends.

Across North River, lights shone yellow from the old, squat hotel named after some forgotten lady of history. Farther, past the bridge and beyond where us kids are permitted to wander, giant houses showed their pale layers like ice-cream cakes—frilly with gazebos and small boats tied to wooden posts sticking up from the water. Low talking brought my gaze back to our side of the river. I spotted, on the concrete path that followed the water's edge, high school guys horsing around on skateboards.

What? C. nudged me with her shoulder.

What what? I asked.

You just said, Hmm.

I said, No, I didn't. You're hearing things.

She huffed. Sure.

I looked at her for a moment, watched sharp wind yank her hair, turn her cheeks a color mine would never go, no matter how cold. She gave me a whole minute before turning those blues, arching her big ol' eyebrows.

What? she said. You have two minutes, then we start back.

How come what I wrote doesn't bother you? I asked. For the zine, I mean.

C. shrugged. You read mine?

I said, Yeah.

Un repartidor wouldn't grab, claw me, silent yanking and yanking.

How come it don't bother you? she said.

You were protecting yourself, I said.

Hey! called a voice from not far away.

One of the skateboarders, skinny, tall, black hair pulled into a bun on top of his head, stepped in close. He looked younger than the others. I recognized him. I clambered off the bench onto the crunchy, icy grass.

Hey, he said again from closer up.

I didn't answer, warily eyeing the two guys trailing him.

You were talking to my sister, said Bun.

He moved still closer. I held ground, shifting slightly so C., who'd also jumped off the bench, was behind me. I let my vision widen, scanning the park while watching Bun and his buddies at the same time. Now that the snow shower had passed, the sky felt huge. One of Bun's friends, a stocky high schooler in high-top Vans, dropped his board, and it landed on the paved path with a *CLACK!* He idly rolled it back and forth with one foot.

What grade he in? asked the other guy, a redhead in a thick hoodie the color of fog.

I answered 'cause I knew he was talking about me, even while he inspected C., who was being unusually silent.

Seventh, I said. And she don't go to school here.

Your name . . . it's Jonah, right? Bun's voice was low, and he let his dangling skateboard drop to the grass.

I didn't correct him. A groan came from the nearby boats rubbing together, the low slap of waves. No dog walkers. No mommies with strollers. No old dude in a tattered, sand-colored Carhartt jacket sitting on an overturned pickle tub, fishing off the dock. Too cold. Too uncomfortable.

I leaned backward into C.'s space to warn her, and in that exact moment Bun rushed forward. I heard C. gasp as I was knocked into her, and then there was a confusion of arms and shouting. I ended up slammed on my back on the bench. My legs flew up and I kicked out, but Bun maneuvered me flat, my head smacking the fake wood. Struggling, I smelled dirt, soggy cigarette butts, and whatever sour thing was on dude's breath.

I've been looking for you, he hissed, spit splattering my face.

Oh, man. Oh, man . . . My hands gripped bony wrists and I felt his pulse pounding. Bun half lifted and slammed me down again. My teeth clacked. Heart: *thumpthumpTHUMP*. Flailing, I tried to knee him in the goods, but he pinned my legs with his in some wrestling move and readjusted to twist my jacket at the throat. We stilled, breathing out cold-air clouds.

Well, said a voice in my head, completely calm. This has been coming for a while.

I heard feet running. More feet chasing. A girl's voice shouted. I figured it must be C. escaping Bun's friends.

Black eyes bored into mine while Bun spoke, teeth expensively straight and white in his brown face.

He said, My sister didn't say, but I know it was you. Saw you at the bookstore. You wanna pick on somebody? Try me.

I swallowed, saying nothing while his face closed in till his two eyes merged into one. More words pushed through his teeth. Oh. I'm too big? How's it feel? Somebody on TOP and you can't get away? How do you like it?

Air left me. Shouts went up. Running again and then what had to be an entire small tree crashed on top of us. I smelled wet bark as twigs scratched, leaves whipped, and slushy ice flew into my eye. The tree lifted and descended again. The third time it nearly knocked him off, but Bun stopped his slide by releasing me to clutch the bench. I wrenched free, rolled, scrambled, and shoved away until I was on my butt on the wet grass, gaping up at the sight of a wild-haired, fierce Concepción.

Girl hoisted a branch like a mace—leaves, twigs, and everything. (She ripped it off a tree?) She thwacked Gideon's brother hard, making him yelp and cover his head. Then she whirled and went after one of the other guys. Gray Hoodie had the nerve to laugh before he took a branch to the mouth. It was an entertaining sight.

High-Tops grabbed at her from behind, but C. shouted HAH! and smashed him. Tree bits flew everywhere. C. darted across the bench's backrest, jumped to the ground, and pointed herself at Bun like she intended to run across and bounce off him, too. When she got close enough, he grabbed the branch and jerked, ripping it from her hands.

I kicked and clawed my way standing, yelling, C.!

It was the first sound I'd forced out since this whole thing started, but C. didn't need me. She darted forward, snatched that branch right back. Bent her knees and rocked smoothly back and forth like a video-game hero. (Who'd've been shocked to see a gold coin rise from nearby tree roots? Not me. *Ping!* Extra life.)

Gideon's brother brought his hands up.

Okay, he said, breathing hard. Okay.

Bun's boys backed up till they made a triangle, with him as the point. Dusting his pants, Gideon's brother bent to retrieve his skateboard where it lay forgotten on its side in the loose dirt and sparkling broken glass. The three of them retreated to the path leading up to the park entrance. Once there, Bun pointed at me and called, STAY the HELL away from my sister!

I waited till they were out of the park before letting my breath *whoooosh*. I flopped backward on the ground like a boneless lump.

Holy crap, I said.

* * *

I fight weones who want to drag me in the street and kill me dead because of what Mamita writes.

From where I was splayed on the ground, I eyed my friend.

De nada, she told me. Also, we're late. Let's not make Tío come get us. That won't be good.

You're not even breathing hard, I accused.

I am, she said as she reached down a hand to help me up.

She wasn't. Girl like glass—smooth.

You hurt? I asked.

Nothing.

Half a block from C.'s house, she staggered to the side. I followed, grabbing for her arm and missing. She sort of tipped over into a nest of weeds and curled like a roly-poly, breathing in choking gasps.

Hey! I shouted, and heard the fear in my own voice.

I turned toward the road but there wasn't a car in sight. Fumbling for my phone, I accidentally knocked it out of sight into the weeds. Crap! I dropped to my knees and started searching for C.'s phone, patting her pockets and thinking how I shouldn't touch her like this, without asking. No phone. Nothing.

My hands hovered over C.'s shuddering body till I took the only option left.

Leaped to my feet and I ran.

I ran ran ran.

DO NOT SEND

THIS IS HOW IT HAPPENED II

After, I threw the candy in a bush.

If anybody found it, I don't know.

Later, eyes shut, I saw her.

Saw myself trying to stop her punching me out.

Girl made a noise between breathing and crying,

like in a movie I once saw at one in the morning.

In it, a dude was over a lady, grunting.

Shoulda turned it. Instead I lowered the sound.

In girl's wrists, I'd felt two tiny hearts beating.

The movie scene I shouldn't've seen? *He* held on.

I let go and she smashed
my face in the street.

I saw stars and blood.
Heard scrambling.

Blind, I shoved and her head smashed back.

She gasped, curled like a potato bug.

It was an accident!

I jumped up, scared.

Candy sack tucked like a football

till I chucked it, I ran.

I ran ran ran ran ran.

Chapter 16
LIES/TRUTHS

Okay, murmured Dad as he settled behind the wheel.

He pulled the door closed and turned to where I hunched in the passenger's seat.

You did good, Jonas, he said in a serious voice. Running to get your friend's brother for help.

Uncle, I mumbled.

Uncle, Dad agreed. Nice guy.

Oh, I thought. Weird. Mom picking me up from C.'s after Mommy & Me Yoga meant that Dad hadn't met Tío, almost never saw C.

Dad stuck the key in the engine and added, Mr. Flores said your friend has been having panic attacks since a kidnap attempt at her mother's in Chile. That's . . . wow. She hasn't suffered one around you previously?

Staring through the windshield at the gray sky, gray houses up and down C.'s narrow street, gray road, I shook my head. The tall grass in her front yard that Tío never bothered much to cut ("buen hogar para los animalitos," he likes to say—good home for the animals) waved and I thought of the crunchy grass at Marine Park. My butt still felt damp from sitting in it and watching my friend take out three guys with a tree branch.

Well, you did good, Dad repeated in the same moment a giant shiver ran up my spine.

He said, Hey. Hey, I know that was hard to see, but she'll be fine, okay? Mr. Flores told you he'll have Concepción text when she's feeling better, remember?

He has no idea, I thought, but I nodded. Dad unwound his black scarf, wrapped it around my neck. He patted my shoulder, then started the car. He pulled out and we drove past the patch of wildness that C. had tipped into.

We're gonna pick up your sister and get some lunch, Dad said. How's Mr. Pizza sound?

When I didn't say anything, he glanced at me and reached over, this time patting my hands folded in my lap. I watched the streets of North River and some of the downtown shops go by. When we passed Mr. Pizza I asked, Where's Rex at?

Oh, she's helping at Soho Stationery this morning, Dad said. Mom needed the afternoon to herself.

We pulled into a parking space near Soho and Dad cut the engine, but before he opened his door, I hurried to speak.

I can't tell you, I explained.

Dad took his hand off the door and we sat with the silence, with the car cooling. *Clickticktick.*

Finally, he asked, What can't you tell me?

I don't want you to— I tried again. I can't . . . I . . . sorry.

The boys and me foolin'. Deer dart. Wolves chase. Candy dropped and rolling away.

I . . . , I tried again.

Mikey's idea. Mikey sucks. Mikey's fault—my fault . . . My fault, too. I clenched my hands.

I need to fix it, I told him.

We can help. Dad braced his elbow against the middle console and leaned into my space, his eyes, like mine, worried.

Your mother and I, he said. We have our struggles, but those struggles aren't you, Jonas. They're not Roxanne. You two are the best— Dad swallowed and leaned back. I looked at my hands and he paused.

You can come to us about anything, Dad said, voice low. Understand? We're on your side.

* * *

I opened the door for Dad. Rex was in Soho, babbling away at Stewart and Anthony. They'd finished the holiday window display, which did this time include a foam-core yeti with motorized arms, designed and built by Stew

Dad waved at Stew and Ant as he called to Rex, Ready for lunch, kiddo?

Her face fell. Stew reached forward and tugged Rex's pigtail.

You've been a huge help today, squirt, he said.

Sunshine-rainbows-ponies. Before Rex's love lasers sizzled me, I ducked into the stockroom to grab her backpack. When I came out, everybody was laughing over something my sister had said. The sleigh bell strap jangled, signaling an actual customer, so Stew went over to help. Ant was fidgeting with his pant cuffs, checking that both sides looked even, and he straightened when I approached.

261

Hey, he said. Stew's been telling me about your typewriter. My gramma had a Royal that she let me bang on when I was Roxi's size.

I admitted, My teacher at school gave me an A on homework that had like a hundred spelling errors 'cause it was typewritered. I didn't know so many people were into them.

Ant laughed. She went to Geek Heaven, huh? That trick work on any of your other teachers?

Dad, who'd been standing near one of the round greeting card racks, idly turning and reading, looked up.

I hadn't heard about that, he said quietly.

Shrugging one shoulder, I located Rex's jacket and held it out for her arms.

Such a good brother. Stew tapped the top of my head as he returned from ringing up a customer.

He noticed that Dad held a greeting card and paused. Buying that?

Dad hesitated, his face running through a few different expressions. Then he said, Sure.

When Dad passed it over, though, Stew kissed the card loudly and handed it straight back.

Blessed! he said.

Uuuuh, Dad said.

On the house. Stew winked at me and I definitely did not wink back. Wasn't sure I approved, especially if this had to do with Mom, which, judging by the way Dad hadn't announced the recipient, probably.

Stewart, Dad tried again. I don't work here anymore.

Uh-huh. Stew leaned over to kiss Rex's cheek.

Ant smiled at Dad and shrugged.

You know what? I said. I think I'm gonna stay here at Soho.

Dad said, You're not on the schedule Saturdays.

Yeah, I said. But since I'm on restriction and won't be in till like Christmas, I wanna finish up that one project I was working on. Can't leave Stew hanging.

Dad said, Have lunch. Maybe you can come back later.

Not really hungry, I lied.

Dad laughed incredulously. You're ALWAYS hungry!

Rex, watching me suspiciously, added, I know *I'm* hungry.

I said, Good. Go with Dad.

Dad said, waving for us to follow him to the door, You're both coming with me.

As she pulled on her pack and trailed Dad, her big eyes asked me, What are you doing?

I wished I could mind-meld with my sister and explain. Even if I got Rex alone in the next ten minutes, it would take serious convincing to keep her from signing a card headed to Mom. Mr. Pizza with Dad and Rex looked less like lunch and more like an argument. I'd had enough fighting for one week.

Widened my stance, planted my feet, thought: They're gonna have to drag me.

Dad warned, Jonas . . .

Stew interrupted, Mr. Abraham, it's cool. We're closing in a few hours. Why don't Ant and I take the little man up on his offer and return him to your condo tonight, fed and watered?

Dad: . . .

Dad: If you're sure.

Ant: We've got this, Mr. A. I'll be here, too, and I can guarantee Stewart won't lose him again.

Stew (frowning): Hey. Not entirely my fault!

Me: I'm not a dog.

Stew (loud-whispering): Shut up and let us help.

*　*　*

I worked and it was easy.

I worked and didn't think about my parents or Mikey or Gideon, and worried only a little about C., who hadn't yet texted.

I worked and Stew and Ant exchanged glances over my head, which I pretended not to see.

I counted, shelved, labeled, and sorted. Answered the phone. Updated the shop Chatter account using Stew's smartphone. Swept the narrow walking path in the stockroom.

I worked until a raspy, surfer-y voice called, STOP.

Looked up to Ant giving me a quizzical look and Stew struggling through a jaw-cracking yawn. Outside the shop's windows, dark and streetlights.

Oh, I said. When'd that happen?

Y'know, said Ant as he folded his bulky arms and leaned sideways against the checkout counter, when you said you wanted to stay, I expected you'd work maybe an hour and then bug off. Didn't know they still made old-fashioned stock boys like you.

Stew bent at the waist and lifted his clasped fists backward in a stretch. He said, I had my money on his stomach eating through his body. Whole new problem to explain to Ms. Adams. Seriously, I had to turn on the Muzak because your gut-growling sounds were disturbing the customers.

That surprised a laugh out of me, and I realized: true, hungry. Checked my phone: two texts from Dad, five from Darius, nothing from C. Little pang in my chest, which I rubbed absently. Lights in the shop clicked off, and then Stew was in my space, herding me toward the door. Ant, carrying my backpack, dropped my jacket over my shoulders.

Ko, Chinese? he asked Stew.

Thai, Stew answered.

While he locked up, I asked Ant, Why were you here all day?

Gonna be gone for a few weeks, he explained. I'm competing up in New Hampshire. Wanted to get some time in with this guy.

When Stew turned around, the smile he held for Ant made my cheeks hot. I looked away down the street and wondered why the two of them could be the way they are while my parents fought. Mikey kept getting pissed about people talking to Charity, but then Darius and Gracie, once they got past the awkward silence and silly notes, smoothed together like peanut butter and jelly. Gideon's brown face popped into my head, her skinny arms, the one earring, silky baby curls—I shut that straight down. Nope.

What's happening with your face? Ant asked as we walked to the restaurant. Fall in a bush?

I touched one of the scratches from C.'s tree attack/rescue and said, Something.

We were shown to a table near the window, and I responded to the texts from Dad but left the rest. I dropped my phone into my lap and raised my head just as Stew was sliding something hidden under his fingers across the table.

You left these when you went out after your friend the other night, he said as he pulled his hand away.

Narrow white strips of label tape sprang back into shape: **WHOOP, thumpthumpTHUMP, FREAK OUT, screaming, candy, stars, the worst thing I ever did, was also the most fun.**

Reads like a poem, observed Ant as he peered from where he sat beside me.

My face felt hot again, for a different reason. Too late now to hide them—no take-backs. What had Stewart thought when he first saw them while I was running after Mikey? Almost didn't want to look at him, but then Stew took the conversation in a different direction.

Your mom hasn't explained much, he said as he poured tea for us three. Just that you're in trouble at school and won't be working at Soho for a while. That explain the black eye?

This isn't a black eye, I muttered. And it wasn't any big deal.

Well, I'm glad to hear *that*, Stew said, yet again raising an eyebrow at Ant. Because a big DEAL might not have you here wearing a shiner and some scratches.

Stop giving the kid a hard time, Anthony said as he pushed up his sleeves, showing off the roots and speckled trunk of the tree tattoo on one arm and, on the other, geometric flowers swirling around the face of a doe-eyed elephant god.

I zoned, watching the street outside the window and wondering where Gideon's brother had gone after he tried to kick my butt.

Ant's voice brought me back. This does read like a poem.

He'd twisted the labels around on the table, nudging the onomato-poetic ones off to the side.

What do you think? he asked.

I read silently: **the worst thing I ever did was also the most fun. Screaming, candy, stars. FREAK OUT.**

These don't belong, I said, and removed some.

We read silently: **the worst thing I ever did was also the most fun . . .**

How's it end? Ant asked, leaning farther into my space so his voice rumbled near my ear.

I took a deep breath, smelling his soapiness and the vinyl tablecloth and sweet spice from the kitchen. I picked up a nearby paper menu, took a pen from my backpack, and wrote in tiny, careful letters: I FELT REALLY FREE. Ripped that off and set it beneath the other lines. The three together, with the last line a jaggy scrap, stopped my breath. I blinked a few times. I cleared my throat.

The worst thing I ever did, Ant started to read aloud, but I put my hand over the poem and shook my head.

It's a haiku? Stew asked.

I love ALL that Japanese stuff, Ant said. Giant robots? Manga.

Our meals arrived then, so I pushed the poem away and applied myself to my pad thai with focus and dedication, as my mom would say. We were winding down when Anthony piped up again.

The worst thing I ever did—I mean so far because I'm practically a baby at age seventeen, he said, grinning/grimacing. NOT fun.

You're twenty-four. Stew rolled his eyes.

As I was SAYING, it's been a while, but I haven't gotten past it. Anthony paused for effect and scratched his beard.

Did anyone get hurt? I asked.

Yeah, he said. Me. Nobody threw any punches. I told a big fat lie and then disappeared. I guess, at the time, I didn't feel like I had a lot of choices. I figured I'd look back and think, no big deal, y'know?

Stewart took a breath, nodding. Little things become big things. Just like that.

Yeah, Ant agreed. The worst was how much I disappointed and terrified my grandfather. He'd raised me, and he swore up and down we were tight, y'know? I should have . . . told him 'stead of running off to a whole other country with that douchebag. They said it's really hard, showing people what you are, and it's true.

Stew reached across the table to lightly tap Ant's big knuckles with a chopstick. He said, And yet, gotta move forward. Freeze and it'll take forever to find your momentum again.

Ant slid my label poem into the center of the table, past our empty dishes. As we waited for the check, Stew and I watched him weigh the ends down with spoons and build a little frame from sugar packets and spilled salt.

Found art, Stew said, smiling.

Ain't it the truth, said Ant.

* * *

After Stewart dropped me at Dad's place and then Dad deposited Rex and me at Mom's, I descended into restriction, which, in our family, is basically solitary confinement except for meals and any book or CD in the house (like anybody listens to CDs).

I slumped in my desk chair, contemplating the labels and scrap of paper Stew, Ant, and I had played with at the Thai place. All my actual zines, except for the first few C. loaned me, had been sucked into the parental abyss. Until I got them back, it'd be hard to find new ideas. Except . . . was that true?

I took out a scrap that my mother failed to confiscate when she steamrolled through here, and flattened it on my desk. Rooting around in my paper stacks, I searched to see if I'd kept any of the notes from way back—before Gideon's brother at the park, before Mikey and the balloons, during the time of wondering and asking around and worrying. Couldn't locate not a one. Too bad, they'd've made GREAT zine material.

I'd settled on meditating on my mollies when my pocket vibrated. Oh, yeah—still had my phone. With the transfer from Dad's car to Mom's house, Dad declining to come in for even a second, and Rex making a fuss over a greeting card, I'd headed straight upstairs to keep out of things. Guess Mom forgot, too, and failed to relieve me of my one means of contact with the outside world.

I spun the phone to read the screen. C.!?

Huh. Unknown number.

???: Ok. Let's talk

Me: Who this?

???: Gideon

A column of heat rushed from floor to ceiling with me at the center. I dropped the phone. Thirty seconds and three deep breaths later, I lifted it from the desk.

???: This Jonas?

Me (saving the number): Yeah

Gideon: You left your number

That was true. I had. There'd been two notes, one for Gideon with my number, another for Mikey that read **BACK OFF**. Turned out fighting fire with fire did nothing more than fire him up.

Gideon: You talk to Darius?

Oh. Right. I'd been ignoring texts except those from my parents. By now, there were probably a dozen from DD.

Me: No

Gideon: We're circling Monday, everybody in VP's office at 8 but we should talk before then. Call now?

The cone of heat I felt suspended in intensified. TALK to her? In PERSON?

Me: Can't. I'm on restriction

Me: I mean punishment. From my parents

Gideon: Monday? Bhaiya's dropping me off at 7

Her brother. Did she know? She had to know.

Me: He wants . . .

Me: Uh. He's gonna talk to me, too?

Me (HOPE not!):

Gideon: No but I

Gideon: Let's just talk about it Monday

Gideon: Bye

I wanted to throw my stupid phone in the trash. I wanted to bite my hand. Start screaming, never stop.

No, Jonas, I told myself. Stop. Breathe deep breaths, like in Mom's magazines.

Be here, I told myself as I huffed with my eyes squeezed tight. Be—

Fish food. I cracked an eye to the strong-smelling container I'd accidentally left open. Lifting the cardboard tube, I thumbed it shut. Then I considered my typewriter: mean, pink zine machine.

The phone buzzed again. This time, it rattled across my knee where I'd placed it, out of sight In Case of Mom. I picked it up.

C.: Alive!

Me: C!

C.: ¡¡ajaja! Tu amiga revoltosa está bien

I snorted and slid down in my chair, grinning weirdly to myself. Yeah, she's about as tough as an ant. Still. Always. The heat that had been suffocating me eased some.

I thumb-typed with feeling, Glad to hear.

C.: :-)

Me: Can't talk long cause don't want Mom to see, but I wanted to say thanks

C.: Anytime

Anytime. *Any* . . . The word jabbed me like an elbow to the brain. I sat straighter.

Me: What you doing Monday at 7:30?

C.: ?

C.: ¿por qué?

* * *

C: How 'bout two? They're short.
I'll send the other later. —JA

This Is How It Happened III

Worst thing I ever did? It was bad, but. Not like I KILLED anyone.

My parents, riled over the black eye, thought I'd been in a fight.

They said, You are NEVER AGAIN going out on Halloween unchaperoned!

I told them, Only fight I had was with a tree
'cause Mikey and me had been chasing each other.

And Dad said, Trees don't fight.

I said, On Halloween they do.

Chapter 17
BOTH SIDES NOW

Early Monday morning a bunch of kids met in the empty playground beside school. Our sneakers and boots scuffled dirt and dried-out, crunched-up prickle balls. By my side, a fire ant. Gideon'd brought her buddy with the soccer legs. We had planned along the same lines, bringing folk to watch our backs. (Once it would've been Mikey beside me.)

We were silent for a bit, watching. I tried not to think how . . . *nice* Gideon looked in a lilac coat to her knees, boots, and that one earring. *Before Halloween, swore she always wore two.*

Gideon's friend, who stood taller than anyone else and glared out of eagle-yellow eyes, unfolded her arms and said sharply, We don't have forever, people. You first!

Before I could speak, Gideon blurted, Don't tell about my brother! Please.

That stopped me. I squinted.

You gonna snitch about candy snatching? C. countered. To, like, people who matter? Adults?

I sucked in a breath. C. figured what I hadn't explained Saturday night over text, when I'd insisted she bike to my school at practically the crack of dawn. Didn't ask her to do anything besides stay nearby in case of, y'know, Bun problems.

Gideon shrugged. I'm way over that.

What? The world swooped around me.

I thought you were the one leaving PO'd notes in my locker, I admitted.

Gideon and friend glanced at each other.

What? I said.

Gideon's buddy said, Maybe you should pick better friends.

Maybe YOU should stop knocking people into walls! I said.

Gideon gave her friend a questioning look. Soccer Legs made a face like, Got me there.

Rolling her eyes, Gideon said, You must know by now that was Mikey.

I said, Did EVERYONE know Mikey was punking me?

Yep, said Legs. And everybody knew you DESERVED it.

I heard a strange sound and glanced over my shoulder to where C. looked a little twitchy, like she wanted to plant a foot on Soccer Legs's face.

Gideon raised her hands to stop us, saying, No time to fight. In circle today, don't say anything about my brother, okay? He can't get in trouble.

Why should I care? I started to say, but C. stopped me with a hand. She said to Gideon, I was at Marine Park, too. I saw. ¿Se disculpará tu hermano?

Gideon's eyes widened. She said, I don't speak—

Just tell him, I said, not to come after me again, and we're even.

Watching us two warily out of her deer eyes, Gideon nodded silently.

Sí, sí, sí, C. said, clapping her hands together. ¿Todo bien?

I answered for everybody. Good 'nough.

*   *   *

Dr. Adeyemo and Gracie were already in the library when I arrived. The before-school crowd must've been turned out to cram for tests and gossip elsewhere. Chairs had been pulled into a circle and, in the middle, someone placed a bright blue rug like kiddies squirm on during free-reading. The rug held a vase of flowers from the librarian's desk, stones painted with words like *believe*, and a box of tissues.

Uh-oh, I thought, taking the open seat between Gracie and Dr. A.

Looking around, I asked, Where's VP?

Vice Principal Hong doesn't usually participate, Dr. Adeyemo said. She'll get a rundown later.

That's strange, I thought. What's being in trouble without VP?

Is the school psych coming? Gracie asked. I thought, she leads these?

Not today, said a voice from the doorway.

Mrs. White hustled in holding a handful of colorful half-sheets. Behind her trailed Charity O'Dell and Mikey.

Mrs. White said, I'll be helping to facilitate, but don't worry, Dr. Adeyemo and I have complete confidence in your ability to work through this.

You and nobody else, I thought as I wiped my hands, already

sweating, against my legs.

Mikey, keeping his head lowered, slumped into the chair across from mine. My heart did a *thumpTHUMP*. Hadn't been this close since last Wednesday. Mikey's eye looked swollen and there were scratch marks on his face, which seemed strange considering I'd thrown punches. My stomach twisted.

Mrs. White stepped into my line of sight and placed a red half-sheet in front of my chair, then moved on to the others. When she was done, she sat and pulled out her phone.

Let's take a minute to breathe, she instructed.

I glanced around. Not even Charity cracked a grin or behaved like anything odd was happening. Dr. Adeyemo's eyes shut so I closed mine, too. (Wouldn't've been too surprised if a fist flew into my face. None did.)

Deep breath in, Mrs. White said. One, two, three, four. And release: one, two, three, four, five, six.

For real, this is the circle-thing kids talk about? I wondered as I tried not to feel stupid. Sittin' and breathin' I could've done at home, following the exercises in Mom's magazines.

A phone alarm chimed and Mrs. White said, Thanks for humoring me. I don't know if you've done mindfulness exercises in other circles, but I needed that transition.

Excellent and appreciated, Mrs. White, Dr. Adeyemo said, making me jump because he was being so quiet I'd forgotten he was sitting next to me.

Teacher smiled, then dove in. She described why we'd come together to sit here like fools (my words) with the goal of "telling our stories to develop a shared narrative around what happened" (her words). Mrs. White had us read the ground rules aloud, beginning on her left.

Charity: Respect the talking stick.

Mikey (mumbling): Speak and listen from the heart.

Dr. Adeyemo: Only your own story leaves the room.

Anyone have questions about those, or need them explained? Mrs. White asked.

I wanted to ask how long we were gonna be stuck in there, but that seemed rude.

Charity raised her hand. I can't say anything about what we talk about?

Of course, I thought. Who but Mikey would bring along the school's biggest blabbermouth?

You can say what you felt or how you now think about something differently, Mrs. White explained. No one, not even us teachers, will share anyone's private details. Make sense?

Charity shrugged. I guess.

Mrs. White continued. Does everyone agree to uphold the ground rules?

She looked around. Everyone nodded.

I acknowledge that this likely feels awkward. Having a structure that everyone understands and can anticipate helps make this space safe enough to say or hear difficult things. Mikey and Jonas will start us off with their experiences. The three of you who are supports can ask questions, as long as you have the talking stick. Finally, you'll decide together how to move forward. Any questions before we begin?

When no one responded, Mrs. White hefted her phone and I watched her swipe open the timer.

I said, We get timed?

Yes, she said, nodding. You'll have five minutes each to describe what happened leading up to now. Don't get too detailed; we won't spend a lot of time on the past. Remember, only the person with the talking stick—she waggled a nubby God's Eye yarn art-stick-thing—speaks. If you need reminding about the ground rules, see the color paper at your feet. Who wants to begin?

Long silence. Mrs. White's blue eyes flicked between our faces. Mikey folded first. When Mrs. White tapped her timer, words poured out, rushing at me. In my head, I threw up a wall that Mikey's accusations crashed against. In real life, Mikey said I never wanted to do anything fun. (What about candy snatching?) I nearly messed things up with Charity. (Can't stand that girl.) He needed my help one time and where was I? (Help him? He was the one who hit me!)

J knows I like to joke, Mikey argued, eyes flashing angrily. He wanted to stop, shoulda said so.

Beepbeep, timer sounded. Five minutes might as well have been a hundred. I sucked in air as, in my chest, a wolf readied to pounce, capture that story, and shred it.

When the talking stick reached me, I snatched it. Opening my mouth to tear Mikey one . . . I stumbled into silence. Mentioning Halloween or candy snatching would bring trouble down on more heads than Mikey's and mine. Gideon's friend who checked me against the lockers, Gideon's brother in Marine Park, Gideon herself—those had nothing to do with Mikey. Mikey and me outside of Soho Stationery: me PO'ed at him for being a weón; him mad I didn't wanna help. Couldn't . . . or wouldn't?

Stuck. I blinked at Gracie, who reached out her hand. I hesitated, glancing at Mrs. White.

It's okay, she said.

Gracie said, I remember you were good friends in September. Did something happen between then and now?

I rubbed the fuzzy bands of white, yellow, and red of the God's Eye in my lap, searching along the strands of the past few weeks. Slowly, it came to me.

Someone left notes in my locker, I said.

Mikey didn't do it! Charity blurted.

Ms. O'Dell, Dr. Adeyemo said. You don't have the talking stick.

The first note, I told them. Said: **I KNOW IT WAS YOU.** Another showed up, and another. I was afraid they'd snowball and bury me.

Weaving around Halloween and Gideon, I told a story with gaping holes. Brought us as far as the stairwell, staring out at my name painted across the hallway—**JONAS DID IT**—before Mrs. White's timer let out a *beepbeep!*

She wiggled her fingers for the stick. The God's Eye passed from hand to hand; I kinda missed it, gave my hands something to do.

Mrs. White said, As we move on to questions, please mind the ground rule: listen and speak from the heart.

Dr. A. raised a finger. When the talking stick reached him, he said,

Listening to your stories, I wondered: how do you know when one person is "serious" versus "playing"?

Friends— Charity started to speak and halted as Dr. Adeyemo reached over with the stick.

Friends should KNOW, Charity said, taking it. My friends, we're close. I mean, sometimes we get mad but it don't last. Nobody goes 'round punching people in the face.

Across the circle, Mikey returned to staring at his hands. Was Charity right? I should be able to guess, hear the tree falling in the forest, spot the Pope in the woods? Hanging with Mikey wasn't like with C., who I could be embarrassed or sad with. Double D'd never raise fists to help, but he'd been keeping me in the loop since suspension. Stew, who paid attention even when I wished he wouldn't, was quick to apologize when he goofed. Even Gracie, who responded to my text request: absolutely.

Mikey didn't admit to stuff. Mikey chased the thrill, no matter what. Mikey wanted to win.

I entered a brief staring contest with Charity till she rolled her eyes and tossed the stick.

Know what, Dr. A.? I said. I *can't* tell the difference. We don't talk. I'm thinking . . . we're not that good of friends.

Long silence. Then Mikey exploded into tears.

My mouth dropped open. Across the circle, Mikey pressed his chin into his chest, sniffing and gasping, arms folded tight. Beside him, Charity O'Dell glared like to set me on fire.

What is WRONG with you? she hissed.

What was wrong with me? My heart was *thumpTHUMPing*, my stomach twisted. What I'd said: true?

Mrs. White cleared her throat. Next, armed with the talking stick, she said, Can you tell us what's upsetting you, Michael?

Charity grabbed for the stick.

Everybody already KNOWS, she said. It's Jonas. Jonas did it.

Screw the talking stick. I demanded, What did I do?

Gracie tilted her head in the opposite direction of her hair and reached out to Charity for the talking stick. She said, I think it's what you're not doing.

What wasn't I doing? Mikey's face remained hidden. Only other wolf in the room? Not so much. Me neither. Like on the playground with Gideon and C., we were wolves and deer both.

Gracie passed the stick to me. It felt fuzzy against my palm. I listened to sniffling, creaky chairs shifting. Smelled shiny books and wooden tables. Windows beyond showed the empty sports field.

My throat tightened. I understood: Mikey and me were no longer the boys we'd been, tearing up that pavement together, fast in the black night.

I said, I know you put those notes in my locker. You thought it'd be funny, but it wasn't.

Across the circle, Mikey dropped his hands. Face more a mess than when we'd battled, he shrugged, then nodded.

I said, Things been going wrong a long time.

I huffed a big ol' sigh. In my ear, Mind-Mama said: Doesn't matter whose fault it was, Baby Bear. Lots of ways in, one path out.

Mikey, I said. I'm sorry.

Truth.

Chapter 18
PATCH THE HOLES

We didn't live fluffily ever after.

After circle, Mikey, Charity, and me were sent to in-school sus-pension to serve our two-day sentence. I sat far, far opposite from Mikey. Somehow, Charity shuffled in late. She held out a note to the white-haired ISS monitor who barely fit behind his desk. Charity, chin up, marched to the rear of the room.

Place was a pale brick box, no windows, no posters of a kitten des-perately gripping a rope. Hang in there. From my seat, I inspected the dark seams and corners. No evidence anyone had ever loved anything here.

We worked. By lunchtime, I could practically smell the anger rising off Mikey. He looked mad enough to come after me. I couldn't be bothered.

I thought, Good luck getting past ISS Sasquatch.

Returning from lunch, Mikey jammed my desk violently, making my pen skid across two lines of a poem and fall to the floor.

That a stress? I wondered over my slashed haiku. Or de-stress? (Ha ha. No pun.)

Ignoring Mikey, I scooped up my pen. The monitor stood, arms folded as he peered over the top of his thick glasses.

Michael Hill, he said to Mikey's disappearing back. That doesn't happen again.

Course it did. Occasionally, Mikey coughed my named loudly and so it sounded like *jackass*. The few times ISS Sasquatch nodded off, Mikey pelted me with rolled paper pellets. He made sure to kick at a leg of my chair whenever he got up for a bathroom pass.

Early in the day, I'd been annoyed, but by day's end, whole thing seemed sad. No excuses left, no hope; the boys, runnin' and laughin' like boogeymen, were done and gone.

By the time the bell rang, I realized: not ALL the boys.

Right, I told myself. Wait and see who's left.

*   *   *

My second day in ISS was just as long and boring, but at least there were fewer daggers stared in my direction and Mikey had stopped trying to knock my desk into Wednesday.

Could be worse, I told myself. I wasn't bumping along in a freight-train car somewhere, my whole life jammed in a backpack as I pretended a wrinkled-up, mouse-bit apple looked delicious.

Before lunch, Mrs. White dropped by with some assignments. She returned last week's science journals with each spelling error circled in sparkly purple ink and dropped a small package in a white paper bag on my desk.

ISS gifts? I said, and shot a glance at ISS Sasquatch, who I expected would growl at me for speaking.

Opening the bag, I pulled out a box holding what looked like tiny movie reels.

I turned the box over, confused. Mrs. White blinded me with her grin.

She said, I noticed your journals were getting light, so here's a recharge. I've missed you in class, Jonas. Get out of hock soon.

Wasn't till end-of-day that I figured out what the rolls were, and then only 'cause ISS Sasquatch took pity and showed me pictures on his phone.

A rare specimen of old tech, he explained as I swiped through insert instructions for typewriter ribbon.

You have one, too? I said, handing him the phone. There's, like, a secret club?

The monitor shook his head. No, son. But ask me sometime about my vinyl collection.

Definitely not, I thought.

* * *

After last bell on Tuesday, VP Hong had me helping the custodian scrub Charity's markering off the floor. Turned out, the reason girl was late to ISS was because they'd made her clean some, too.

On my knees, I sprayed the nasty-smelling stuff and gripped a wooden brush with my too-big gloves. Two sets of shoes squeaked into view. I looked up and there they stood, pinkies linked.

Hey, I greeted Darius, sitting back on my heels. I added, Sorry for not responding to your texts. I had a lot going on.

Darius shrugged, but I wasn't sure what he meant.

Gracie, her braids pulled up into an enormous bun that reminded me of the baskets people keep cobras in, said, Word in the office is y'all got a week of community service.

I wiped my brow with my arm and said, Here's hoping they don't make us serve together.

Darius patted his 'fro with his free hand. You not talking to Mikey still?

What do you think? I asked, spraying that nasty stuff over the mostly faded **S** in my name, ratcheting up my "elbow grease," as the custodian called it.

I think you do a lot of not-talking, Darius observed.

I laughed, said, Pots and kettles, Double D.

He huffed, then grinned. Trees in the woods?

This time, I grinned, all teeth. Popes.

Gracie gave us a weird look. She said, Coming to Mr. Pizza later?

Nah, I said. They have more stuff for me to clean.

Darius hesitated. I can stay. Got another pair of gloves?

I stood so I could pull off one glove and pat his shoulder.

No, man. I'm good, I said. Then I spotted Dr. Adeyemo at the other end of the hall. Hey, you guys should—

Darius's hair whipped back, his feet moved so fast.

Text me! he called as they got the heck out of range.

❋   ❋   ❋

Tuesday's Dad Night, but Mom seems to have stopped caring about that and appeared at the condo right when we were arriving from the supermarket.

Here we go, I muttered under my breath.

Rex narrowed her eyes in a superior way, still gloating over my aiding her cause by giving them a reason to fight so hard, they'd boomeranged back toward each other. Since the shouting match in the driveway, plus the card from Dad, which my sister (the traitor) told me she'd signed, the parents made real, on-the-calendar plans to "see someone together." I assumed they meant like a therapist, and no way did I approve. Rex approved 200 percent.

After we put away the groceries, Dad parked Rex on the couch with the tablet, giant headphones lengthened to fit over her big, loose 'fro. Then he and Mom nudged me upstairs.

I sat on Dad's bed, which was already made up for me. Dad took the floor. Mom blocked the door.

What's going on? I started to ask.

Dad held up one of the zines Mom had confiscated a few days ago: A Young Person's Guide to Consent for Every Body

Oh, no, I said.

The Talk. My parents said a lot of Words Related to Bodies. It was awful and embarrassing. I barely survived. When I felt two days from the Zombie Apocalypse, Mom decided she'd wreaked enough havoc and stole Rex away for a late dinner out.

What? I complained to Dad. I have ISS and you make me listen to you and Mom talk about gross stuff, and THEN Rex gets to go out for apple pie à la mode?

Dad raised an eyebrow at me as I dragged behind him into the kitchen.

He said, It wasn't that bad, little man. You and your sister have known how sex works since you were babies. We want to be sure you understand that intimacy is more than—

I clapped my hands over my ears and sang, Lalala!

Dad handed over the zines, which he'd rolled and stuffed in his back pocket.

He said, Here's an idea. Ring your friend Concepción, see if she wants to come for dinner.

That was strange, considering how we'd spent half an hour going over "healthy boundaries" and what I shouldn't yet do with "anyone of any gender expression or sexual identity." Not gonna mention that.

Thirty minutes later, C. stepped into the foyer, head swiveling, eyes bright and curious. Long as we'd known each another, C. hadn't visited either of my places.

Jonas, why don't you put your friend's coat in the closet? Dad called down the stairs, like I wasn't his son, hadn't already held my hands out to take it.

Hi, Mr. Abraham! C. yelled.

Dad stuck his head around the wall and clacked a set of metal tongs. I hope you like frittata?

C. held up a covered plate. I brought leche asada that Tío made. Hope you like custard-y pudding stuff.

Pudding stuff is fine, I informed her. But your socks are mismatched.

¡No, poh! C. lip-farted. ¡Ellos son bacán! They're perfect!

Chapter 19
REVOLUTION

On the night of my first day back to regular school, I felt tired and not-tired. Slogged through the day with other kids eyeing me like I'd come down with something hideous enough to keep their distance, but then they also wanted to see the spots.

Avoiding Mikey, it turned out, was a LOT of work; he was in four classes with me and Darius, who was so far refusing to give either of us up in the divorce. Then, during lunch, I tried to concentrate on the new handheld games Aaron brought over to trade, but Mikey yakked as loud as possible with Charity's twittering crew and kept calling DD over to his table for stupid stuff. Aaron caught me glaring across the room and tilted his head, looking between us. He didn't comment. Neither did I, though it was probably obvious with all that steam pouring out my ears.

In my quiet, peaceful bedroom I lay on my stomach on the floor and looked through the folder I kept my zine attempts in. Had to laugh at myself how deep into this project I'd fallen. When C. visited at Dad's, she promised that, on Saturday, we'd finally put the whole zine together. I had to admit, kinda excited about seeing the finished project. Better than any glued-up twig chart.

I'd produced a lot on my own, too. Some of my attempts were typed, some scrawled. A bunch were poems.

English teacher'd be proud, I thought. I'll never show her.

Contrary to popular opinion, I didn't keep all the candy for myself.

The worst thing I ever did was leave my sister at Mr. Pizza. She was five.

My best candy-snatching experience happened in sixth grade.

I don't know why I did it.

Looking at my pages spread out was kinda embarrassing. Reading about candy snatching over and over, I remembered how wild it'd been—the chase, the capture. Speed and agility forever, like I'd never run out. Like me and the boys wouldn't get old or mess up—or get caught.

Having your stuff stolen's not fun, but I bet some kids would admit the experience was exciting: Big Bads pounding the pavement after Squealing Littles. Kids had other choices, after all, like hanging 'round the lumbering herd of parents toting babies and toddlers dressed up like skunks and sugar peas.

Another choice was to stand ground and fight. Some kids wildly swung flashlights and kicked. Mostly kids ran. Running was FUN! Even Gideon ran. And when I caught up it wasn't like she got cornered, whole neighborhood to duck away and hide in.

It had been fun at the time. All these weeks out, *so* much less fun and more kinda . . . awful.

I wavered between what it felt like to run like wolves and admitting things had gotten out of control. I took a breath and sat up, then I arranged and rearranged the haiku labels and the jagged scrap. When it didn't lead where I'd hoped, I moved to the desk and ran my fingertips lightly across the typewriter keys, listened to soft zipping like any normal keypad. Breathing in that oil scent, the metal dust, I fed the machine fresh paper.

Rex's red-handled safety scissors caught my eye, and I paused to dig out the zine that C. had loaned me. *Snip-snip* and a strip of tape. "A Recipe for Disaster" was now displayed over my desk. Swimmy and Alex drifted toward the shadow, lips moving like they were reading silently. I considered putting up my haiku, but Mind-Jonas stopped me.

Worst thing I . . .

The worst thing I'd ever done, so far: Was it candy snatching or seeing Gideon curled on the ground? Maybe the worst thing was a kid wishing his parents would finally give it up, or being the Reason no matter how much those parents argued: We love you kids. This is between us adults.

I wheeled my chair closer to the desk and straightened my spine like in the yoga magazines, picturing a balloon pulling at the top of my head.

Maybe the worst thing was hitting Mikey when he went too far.

I'd gone too far, too.

* * *

Stop looking at me like that, I complained. I didn't expect all these—you never mentioned other people!

C., who was getting a whirlwind tour of the Adams/Abraham homesteads, sucked her teeth.

What are you saying? she countered. Don't you remember the snow? The layers?

We settled on the floor in the den (aka Mom's home office). Mom vacated after she showed us down after dinner. I could tell she was curious, but since she and Dad had already said their piece, there wasn't a good enough reason to pry. Rex, on the other hand, didn't need excuses. Thankfully, her school-night bedtime is eight.

Go upstairs, brat, I commanded.

She responded by sticking one of my drafts in her mouth and shaking her head, growling.

Oh my god, Rex! I shouted while C. fell over laughing.

Roxanne! Mom called from upstairs. Did you brush your teeth?

My sister dropped the now-soggy paper. Standing up in her footie jammies, she waved at C. and said, ¡Buenas noches!

Buenas tardes, Roxita. C. smiled and wiggled her fingers.

When my sister was gone, I told C., This is a LOT.

In my hands was a ton of badness. Art, drawings, charts, and . . . bumpy, typewritten pages. (Other typewriters!)

When did you get to know so many people? I asked, trying to ignore the voice that was telling me how much better the pages in the folder looked than the half-baked stuff I'd turned in.

At the same time, another part of my brain started spinning design ideas, like what if I make a deer/forest collage backdrop for "This Is How It Happened"?

You heard of this thing called the internet? C. smirked.

She said, I put out a call. Kids in my homeschool group sent some; lot are from online. So many, I might need to do a website, like you said. It would cost too much money to print everything.

I said, I thought you didn't use the internet.

What are you worried about? She snorted. You made enough to fill a whole zine.

*   *   *

By Friday, I had the fever. Revolución? Sign me up!

In the den, despite my parents' restrictions (which never extended to learning and makin', let's be honest), C. had the place papered with the worst thing anyone ever did times, like, fifty.

We dug in, comparing and stacking. C. had brought over Tío's crazy-fast scanner that he uses at research libraries, and I swear the temperature in the basement rose due to all the scanning. At some point, Mom dropped by to make sure we hadn't died or started making out. C., consumed by folding blank sheets of paper this way and that according to the instructions in her zine how-to book, never looked up. I waved distractedly. Mom slipped away again.

How can you read all these and not hate people? I asked C. (half meaning my zine pages / me).

C. hadn't said much about what I'd written. I knew it wasn't that she didn't care, since she's all about the People and Doing Right (except when she's about biting little girls and fleeing South America).

She said, I had no idea I'd get *this* many. Even Juan-Rupert sent one—not tellin' you which!

A pause. She added, People are jerks and a lot of the times they're not sorry. But . . . read a bunch and you get it, sí poh? You meet yourself . . . maybe?

We returned to our tasks. A few of the zine submissions were too taped and glued to go through the scanner without getting messed up. I put those aside and checked through the scans on C.'s laptop to make sure things looked good, the file types correct. Finished with that, I collected the scanned pages back into the plastic folder she'd brought. An idea bloomed.

When this is finished, I said, I bet Stew would let us print copies at Soho, and then we could take some to Robin at North River Books.

C. clapped her hands and said, Let's! Tío Rodrigo said, since this is for school, he'll pay postage and we can mail 'em to everyone who sent stuff in.

You're getting credit for homeschool? I asked. There's no deadline, though, right?

C. laughed, which I took as: no, poh.

I said, So, if . . . it feels like a story's missing? If I wanted to invite . . . ?

Your friend? She pointed to her own eye. Who hit you?

Oh, hell no, I said.

Even if Mikey and me weren't done FOREVER, dude needed a solid chunk of Jonas-Free. DD'd be game, Aaron'd laugh in my face. My mind kept churning. Before Tío Rodrigo arrived and I returned to the Restriction Zone, I searched out a certain number who'd texted me this week.

I thumb-typed: There's this thing a friend is making. I see you read. Maybe you like to write?

I hit send.

WHAT IT LOOKS LIKE
(BUT IS THAT WHAT IT IS?)

Worst thing I ever

Did was also the most fun

I felt really free

    Wolves run. One stops. He

    watches but he doesn't no-

    tice: deer sees him, too.

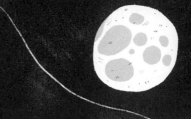

Chapter 20
WHAT WOLVES SEE

Gideon didn't respond.

Forget it, I told myself. You did what you could.

Mom says things take time. Dad says keep moving forward. My phone had nothing to add—still confiscated. No Darius keepin' in touch, no zine production updates from C., and of course nada from Mikey.

During the week things seemed back to normal except that Mikey had Moved On so hard it was like I'd stopped existing.

Saturday happened. Mom agreed to drop me at C.'s on the way to yoga, long as I agreed not to leave the premises. (After what happened last time? No way.) Tío seemed happy to see me—which was a bit weird since, last we hung out at her place, his niece had a panic attack in a bush. He set us up on the cold indoor porch with warm empanadas de queso in a little wicker basket, cozy under a checkered kitchen towel.

C. moved the solar system over so it sat against the backdrop of sheet-covered furniture, except for Earth, which held forth on the rocking chair. I'd make a joke about that if I could scare one up. When C. saw me trying, she patted my cheek, called me cachorro triste, and set me working on the final few zine pages that hadn't been scanned.

What's this? C. asked as she picked up the folder I brought with me.

Nothin', I said. Some ideas I had.

A cover? she asked.

I replied, I was just playing around with the typewriter.

She said, I can use it?

I glanced at the few pages of haiku collage attempts she held in her thin fingers. I said, I guess.

The sun slanted across the porch. C. fussed around, setting up the screens she'd been working on so many weeks ago. At first, I stood back 'cause I wasn't down to splatter ink around the porch like last time, but seeing the two-color cover she'd designed come together, I started itching to try it. Just one, y'know?

C. showed me how to set the screen down on the paper, (carefully) squeeze in a blob of blue ink above the image, and then press, press the long rubber squeegee and chase that ink, lay it out flat, pull it toward my knees. I carefully picked up the squeegee and set it aside, raised the screen to gaze down at the blue title: *Últimx Confesadx*.

The worst, confessed. We all had, each writer. We wrote words or a poem or made funky, ripped-paper art about THAT thing, THOSE things. What we did but shouldn't've. We (I) said what had gone right, knowing it was wrong. Some people go to church and say it was me / I did it / I'm sorry. Not me. Even if I was that kind of kid, I wouldn't take back all those hours with the boys, beating the blacktop. We were WILD. Our shouts made the moon stare down. Made the moon know who we were.

Gideon was part of the story, but she wasn't the whole story. I wasn't her whole story either. Before everything happened—ISS, restrictions, the punches with Mikey—I didn't think there was more worth telling or knowing about Halloween or snatching. I froze the frame: Gideon the deer, Jonas the wolf. Frozen stuff melts, and then there's motion. It's science. You can't stop it.

Chewing loudly, C. nudged me with her elbow and said, It's gonna dry. ¡Listo!

Snapped out of my thoughts, I shuffled on my knees to the second screen and laid down the red. When I put the screen to the side and held up the completed cover, a blue title and red image shone wet, waiting to dry. When it did, we'd turn it sideways, fold it in half, and stuff printed-out pages inside. Zine taco.

Nice, C. commented over her shoulder, not actually looking.

Seemed she was working on something secret-y, so I didn't bother her. I became a machine. C. cranked the tunes and I applied myself: blue to screen one; squeegee; red to screen two; squeegee; stand up and hang it with clothespins on a long twine tacked between the two farthest porch windows. Some of the papers curled and I let 'em. Outside gray, gray, but on C.'s porch, red and blue on repeat.

A text from Mom said she'd swing by in ten. We were mostly done anyway. I opened the door to carry the screens out to the kitchen and was blown back by a woman loudly rapping in Spanish over fast drums. Tío intercepted before I reached the sink and chacha'd me by the shoulders to the basement door. I went downstairs to wash up in a deep plastic sink with a stiff brush and powder that came in a cardboard tube with a chick on it. Leaving the screens propped, I went back up to help C. straighten the sun porch, but she slapped my hands away from the ink bottles.

Ah-ah, she said. No time. Here. Look at this before you go.

Handed me a booklet folded into a square from one sheet. The cover was what I'd created, reduced. Three lines of haiku slanted up with white space around them, an effect created by label tape stark against a leafy background I'd made by cutting up photos from Mom's yoga magazines.

C. was telling me, I didn't mess with your original.

That wasn't why I stopped breathing for a sec. On the cover, my words. Inside, my words . . . so many and so tiny. My name didn't appear anywhere on or in it, anónimo, but Jonas Adams Abraham was all over the thing. Running, laughing boogeyman Jonas with his boys and those deer, leaping. Smoke, fire, wolves. With everything that had happened since, Halloween felt like a year ago.

My eyes, joining my throat and my heart in fightin' me, burned. I swallowed and then gave up, let the storm blow me off balance.

¿Necesitas un abrazo? C. asked, like she was the one who'd read *Consent for Every Body*, and opened wide her skinny arms.

I could choose, or not. It was more than I'd given Gideon, less than I'd received from Mikey. Didn't know I needed to be doing it till I did. Wrapping my arms tight around C., I breathed in deep. Girl smelled like fresh dough and dry winter grass. C.'s hook nose pressed into my shoulder as I snugged her closer. Nobody saw but me and her.

＊　＊　＊

VP Hong's voice asked, Everything all right, Gideon? Jonas?

We stood in place with our eyes locked: Deer / wolf. Wolf / deer? Wolf / wolf?

It was after last bell on Monday. I'd been at my locker selecting books. Heard the soft scuffing behind me and turned and saw her. Like practically every time our eyes met, stuff happened. My heart: *BAMbam*.

Gideon, unsmiling, said:

And then I said:

And Gideon added:

So finally, I confirmed: You'll do it? The zine?

Gideon (snorting): I don't know why I would. We've never done a project together, even for school. Plus what's a zine?

Me: Lemme show you.

Which was when VP Hong stepped in 'cause I guess we looked suspicious, me not even a week out of ISS and Gideon only recently not giving me the flaming hairy eyeball for something no teacher knew to suspend me over, and no other person could confirm went down, end of October.

I had nothing to say, but girl did. Dark-eye serious, unafraid, she volleyed VP's question with a quick We're okay; reached over and shut MY locker with a soft click. VP stepped back.

Well, she said, folding her hands and nodding. I trust you're aware it's our goal for students to continue developing socio-emotionally, which includes learning from past mistakes and moving forward together, modeling North River's values: caring, respect, responsibility, and growth.

We blinked, momentarily blinded by the pinstripes and VP-talk. I tried a smile. Gideon went with stone-face. VP winked and crisply strode off to pester kids into leaving the building faster.

Girl and I beat it out of school, Gideon leading the way with her loose hair sliding over her shoulder. In the cold and wind, it blew up and out like a flag, and I watched, thinking how, before Halloween, that would not have been something I'd notice.

The sun bit hard as we moved to the side yard, our feet crunching mostly powdered leaves as we passed idling cars and heard shouting kids and the rattling rumble of buses pulling into traffic. We paused near the low wall separating the two parts of the playground.

We didn't know each other. Now it seemed we should. First, I had to introduce myself.

Feeling silly, I reached into my back pocket and pulled out the minizine C. had made. My only copy, even though I had the full-size original. As I passed it over, my hand trembled. Girl took it, and I watched her bowed head, her slim brown hands as she flipped the few pages.

This is a zine, I said. I wrote it. My friend, uh, that short girl you saw the other day, last Monday? She helped. She's kind of a master and turned what I made into this lil' baby zine.

I forced myself to stop talking. Let the art do it. Or not.

Gideon's head rose, eyebrows pulled in.

I don't get it, she said. Is this about you . . . stealing candy? Why did you write it like this? Who's it for? It's weird.

Is it weird? I asked, heart dropping, dropping.

It's TOTALLY weird, said Gideon. This is supposed to be me? I'm not a weakling . . . a *deer*. You're telling it wrong. Maybe I should write my *own*.

My heart stopped plummeting, belly loosened. Girl nailed it. Absolutely, completely, 100 percent correct.

I nodded. Half laughing, breath puffing a cloud, I said,

You should.

Acknowledgments

I confess Big Gratitude to the people and places who prompted and supported the creation of this book. A novel is a thing that touches the mundane and the extraordinary, remixes them into windows and doors that we throw open, letting in the light of new suns, new stars. In my life, my parents and brother, aunts and uncles, and little cousins are the stars; my partner, our art-friends, and our found family, including the furry ones, are the suns; and readers I haven't yet met, you are the wide sky, you are the galaxies. I am waiting for you, welcoming you. Come on in.

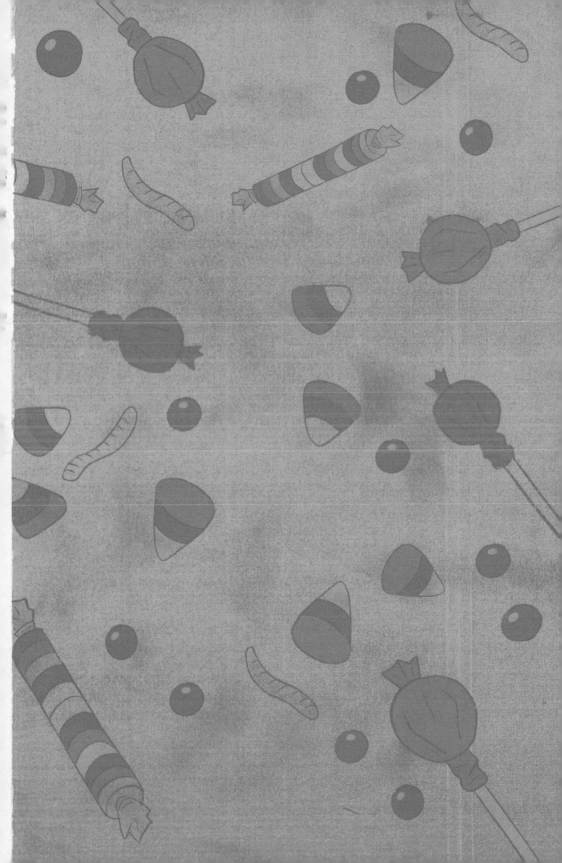

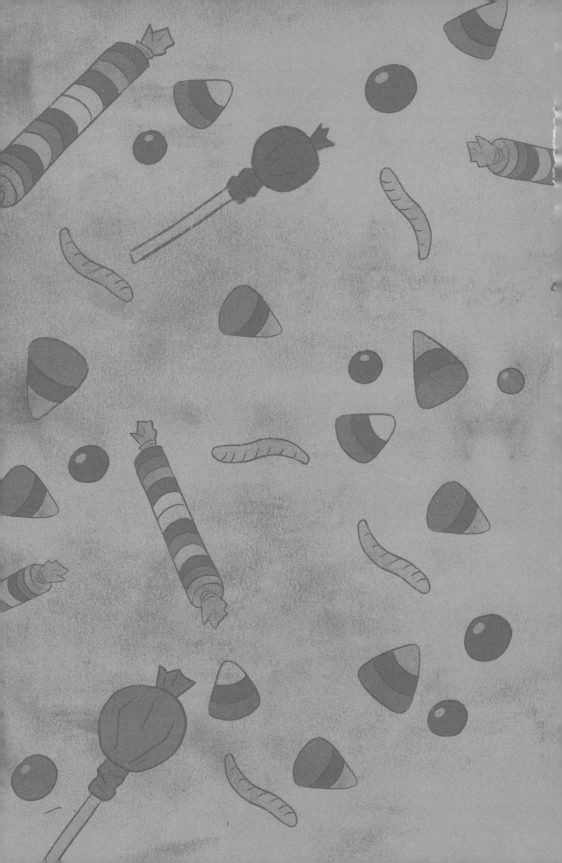